ERIKA TAMAR

FAIR GAME

HARCOURT
BRACE &
COMPANY

SAN DIEGO
NEW YORK
LONDON

Requests for permission to make copies of any part of the work
should be mailed to: Permissions Department,
Harcourt Brace & Company,
8th Floor, Orlando, Florida 32887.

Library of Congress Cataloging-in-Publication Data
Tamar, Erika.
    Fair Game/Erika Tamar.—1st. ed.
        p.   cm.
    Summary: High school senior Laura Jean is shocked when
    the school jocks are accused of gang-raping a retarded girl
    and her boyfriend Scott appears to be involved.
    ISBN0-15-278537-X; ISBN 0-15-227065-5 (pbk.)
    [1. Rape—fiction.   2. High schools—Fiction.
3. Schools—Fiction. 4. Mentally handicapped—Fiction.]
I. Title.
    PZ7.T159Fai   1993
    [Fic]—dc20   93-3248

Designed by Lori J. McThomas

First edition
A B C D E

Printed in Hong Kong

For anyone who has ever been
"the other"

Special thanks to Ray Sapirstein, who
said it was important and encouraged
me to start; to Patricia Lakin, who was
there every step of the way; and to my
wonderful editor, Karen Grove

FAIR
GAME

LAURA JEAN

My letters are already folded and in the envelopes, ready to go, but I take one out and reread it again. I want to be sure it sounds right.

May 24

Letters to the Editor
Long Island Press
65 Railroad Drive
Mineola, NY 11501

Dear Editor:

I am writing to you because of the false things you're printing in your articles about the high school athletes of Shorehaven.

I've known Scott Delaney for a long time. He's a nice, regular guy, and he's never been in any kind of trouble. He didn't commit any crime. It's very unfair to put his and the other boys' pictures with "Jock Assault" headlines. You ought to get the facts straight.

Everyone knows the girl was available to anybody and that she'd been "servicing" half the football team. I have witnesses who saw her doing Charlie Goren in the back of the balcony of the school auditorium, and they're willing to say so. What happened that day— she wanted it, and I guess that's her business. Even her own mother doesn't want to press charges.

I'm not writing her name because I know you're going to black it out. All the papers have been real careful about not printing her name, but you don't think twice about putting in all the boys' names and pictures and interviews about them behind their backs, and that's not right. I thought this was still America, where you're innocent until proven guilty.

You and the rest of the papers and the TV are making a big mountain out of a molehill, and I wish you'd stop. You're making a very good high school and a nice town look bad. You're spoiling the end of senior year, which was supposed to be the best time, for a lot of

regular guys and their friends, and you're doing
it just to sell papers. It isn't fair.

Yours truly,
Laura Jean Kettering
58 Sycamore Road
Shorehaven, New York 11051

P.S. I am sending this same letter to the *New
York Times,* the *New York Post,* and *Newsday.*

It's the best I can do. I rewrote it a couple of
times; it took a while to come up with "available"
and "servicing." What I really wanted to say is
the girl's a slut and she's been giving out blow
jobs, but they won't print it if I don't keep it
polite. I really wanted to rage and rant at all the
reporters that are circling around town like vul-
tures, hounding us, and writing lies.

I put stamps on the envelopes and seal the
flaps. Mom will have kittens if they publish it,
but I don't care.

When the whole thing got out, the first thing
she said was, "Keep out of it, Laura Jean. I don't
want you getting mixed up in this."

"But they're crucifying those guys. You know
Scott is—"

"Listen to me. Don't talk to anybody." I guess

Mom's embarrassed; all her friends know Scott is my boyfriend.

Mom and Dad treated Scott like family, and I think it stinks that they're so ready to drop him now.

Dad found me crying one morning.

"Scott is a nice guy, Daddy," I said into his shoulder. "You know he's a nice guy."

He patted my back, kind of awkwardly, like he didn't know what to say. Finally he came out with "He got caught in a dumb mistake. But it's—just back off, baby. We want you to stay away from him."

So much for loyalty. I'll say this—at least the kids at school are behind the guys one hundred percent. That snitch is getting his ass kicked just about every day.

I don't know that my letter will help, but I've got to do *something*, at least until I think of something else. Scott looks shaky. He doesn't say so, but I can tell he's scared, and that's making me crazy.

I'm going to stand by my man. I always liked that Tammy Wynette song. Scott used to tease me about country music—"shit-kicker music," he called it. I'm not into all that metal stuff he likes, so I'd play my Patsy Cline tapes—I love

"I Fall to Pieces" and "Sweet Dreams" because they're so emotional—and Scott would start this stupid yodeling. It got me so annoyed. That and the raisins. Raisins revolt me; I think they're withered, rotten grapes. Scott thought that was funny as hell, and he kept trying to get me to eat them. Like he'd pop raisins in my mouth when I wasn't expecting it. Once I almost puked. Or he'd start acting like one of those dancing raisins, singing "I Heard It Through the Grapevine." Sometimes, if something struck Scott funny, he wouldn't let it go, like a dog worrying a bone. But it was just little things. We really got along so great; we hardly ever had fights or anything.

God, I'm remembering everything like it's all in the past. It can't be! I mean, guys like Scott Delaney or Bob Dietrich or John Masci don't go to jail . . . But I'm scared. I'm scared. Well, no matter what, I'll stand by my man.

Just a couple of months ago, I'd never have imagined that song could take on so much meaning. Back in April, when I didn't even know how good the ordinary, normal day-to-day was.

LAURA JEAN

APRIL IN SHOREHAVEN IS ALWAYS BEAUTIFUL, SO I guess the forsythias and daffodils and dogwoods were blooming. Mostly, they're just there and I forget to notice. Except for the time Mom drove me down Lloyd Hill Road and said, "Look at that, Laura Jean. Look at all that color." Or maybe that was later, when the azaleas came out.

Anyway, that day in April, I was standing in the kitchen, a whole bunch of schoolbooks weighing down my arms, ready for school. There's a big magnolia in our backyard, and you can see it through the glass of the kitchen door. I don't remember if it was in bloom then; I was busy arguing with Mom and feeling more frustrated every minute. I do remember the exact date: April 16. That's because Scott was supposed to get an answer from Dartmouth on April 15, and they had come through for him with a full scholarship. He'd sounded so excited when he called and told me.

That was partly why I wouldn't let Mom brush me off.

"Go on to school. We'll talk about it later," she said.

"But I don't want to wear the bridesmaid's dress!"

"It's a perfectly beautiful dress, Laura Jean."

"I know, I know. But not for the Fling!"

"You're going to be late for school."

"I don't care. Mom, Pat's giving me a ride to Lord & Taylor's this afternoon, so if you'll just—"

"For God's sake, it doesn't have to be this afternoon. I'll think about it."

"The stores get picked over early." It wasn't just because of the Fling; St. Mary's and Manhasset had their proms coming up, too. "I want to go this afternoon! There'll be nothing left!"

"I don't have any cash to give you right now."

"Oh, great!" I stomped to the door. "So we can't go today!"

Mom was smiling the kind of smile that says all these little teenage things are cute and unimportant. "You know, Scott will like you just as much in the bridesmaid's dress."

That made me so mad I couldn't speak.

"Have a good day," she called after me.

Sure, terrific. I wore the stupid bridesmaid's

dress for my sister Anne's wedding last year. Pastel blue, Anne's color, not mine. I knew exactly what Mom was thinking: Why spend perfectly good money when you already have . . . The dress was OK, but Scott had seen me in it already, and it wasn't *sensational*. She didn't understand why I had to be memorable at the Fling. I couldn't talk to her about that.

The thing was, if you loved someone, you were supposed to be happy for him. And I'd been going through all the hoping with Scott.

"Remember when the American hockey team beat the Russians? Winter Olympics, 1980, Lake Placid?" Scott was so excited. "This coach I met at Dartmouth—he was on that team!"

"1980? We were just kids then."

"Well, you must've heard about it, the Miracle Team? We've got the tape somewhere—I'll show you . . ."

I guess Dartmouth was the best for hockey, and I wanted the best for Scott, I honestly did. But when it had really happened . . .

See, I'm not beautiful; Scott is better-looking for a guy than I am for a girl. My hair is nice when I work on it—it used to be mud brown, but I made it auburn this year—and I have nice eyes, but my nose has a bump. It's not horror-movie terrible—my folks aren't about to shell out for a nose job—but it's far from perfect. People talking about me would say I'm cute and have a good personality. I knew Scott loved me, so it wasn't something I worried about that much, but now he'd be going so far away . . . I needed to look new and glamorous for the Fling, and I knew exactly what I wanted—something strapless with a long tight skirt slit up above my knee, in shiny black—and I'd get my hair done up in a French twist. That night, that one night, I wanted to reach for beauty and burn a picture into his mind he'd remember forever and ever.

I'd been planning to add all my savings from Foodtown to whatever Mom gave me. I work at Foodtown three afternoons a week, and by the end of my shift, I'm brain dead. It wouldn't be so bad if I actually had to memorize the prices to ring them up or do some mental subtraction to make change, but it's all bar codes and computerized. I would have liked something that demanded more of me, something where I could be proud of doing a good job. Waitressing at least required personality, but Dad said he didn't want his daughter serving people. It paid better, too, and I didn't see anything wrong with service, but it wasn't worth an argument. Maybe Dad would help me out for the Fling. He was always bragging about his stable of beautiful Kettering women. When I was little, I told Mom I didn't want to be in a stable like a horse. Mom laughed and said that means Dad loves his four girls a lot and isn't disappointed about not having a son, the way a lot of men would be.

I'd left my wristwatch on the kitchen counter. I had no idea what time it was; I'd probably been arguing with Mom for too long. I started walking faster. I hoped Scott would still be waiting on the corner of Sycamore and Oak. I liked walking to school with him in the mornings, when the whole crowd of guys wasn't around. They were a great bunch of guys—except for Mike Clay, who had a really foul mouth—but it was nice to be alone with Scott.

Good, he was still there.

"Are we late?"

"Don't think so," he said. "Anyway, I can show up at noon if I feel like. I've got it made in the shade."

"So you're really psyched?" I was continuing our phone conversation from the night before. We did that a lot, just continue a conversation from where we'd left off the night before, and the guys would laugh and say, "Where did that come from?" I liked to think Scott and I were kind of telepathic.

"Hell, yeah!"

"Me, too." I tried to sound happy.

"You should've seen me go to the mailbox yesterday, holding my breath, shaking in my boots. Shit, Dietrich had all kinds of offers, since *January*, like football's the only game in town. I was kinda pissed. But when I felt that nice thick envelope—oh, man!"

"It's so far away, though."

"Not that far. Listen, I can fly home on weekends. I bet they give me transportation money, all kinds of perks 'cause"—he stopped and posed in front of me, thumbs up, big smile—" 'cause I'm THE FASTEST SLAPSHOT IN THE EAST!"

"I won't get to see your games." I didn't care if my toes froze off at the outdoor arenas. I'd just about explode with pride when he'd swoop down the ice, graceful as any dancer, with everyone yelling "Go, Delaney!" I only missed one game this year, when I had the flu. I guess football season was more exciting in a way, with the whole town coming out and the cheerleaders and the band and everything, and I'd cheer him on there, too, but mostly everyone would be yelling for Bob: "Die-trich! Die-trich!"

"I'll phone and give you the blow-by-blow," Scott said.

I forget where I heard that a drowning man sees his whole life pass in front of him. I was seeing the partying after the football games, the guys loud and flushed with victory, the laughs and the noise and everyone crowding around Dietrich, Clay, Masci, Goren, Lopez, and the Delaney brothers—Tommy and Scott. Scott.

"It won't be the same," I said. *If only we could go to Stony Brook together*, I thought. But that was silly; the SUNY schools weren't hockey powers.

"I'll call and write a lot," he said. "And there's vacations and summers."

"It won't stay the same," I said. My voice started breaking and, all of a sudden, right in the middle of Sycamore Road, I found myself crying.

"Come on, L.J." Scott looked uncomfortable. He put his arm around my shoulder.

"I know . . . this is so dumb." I rubbed my hand across my eyes. "Sorry."

"We've still got the whole summer," he said.

"It's going to end."

"The summer," he said. "Not us."

Please God, not us.

"Come on, L.J. It'll be okay."

I could feel him watching my face as we went past the patch of woods near the school. I wasn't going to cry again. I wasn't. Not in front of him. Scott always said he liked that I was feisty. That was about the first thing he said to me. "Feisty."

Way back in seventh grade, when all the elementary schools emptied into the one junior high, all the girls got crushes on Scott Delaney and Bob Dietrich. Maybe more on Bob, because he's truly movie-star handsome, the kind of blond good looks that everyone goes for. But for me, it was only Scott, from the very first time I saw him. He was in my homeroom and his dark eyes were so alive and sparkly. That's when the boy-girl parties started—mostly it was the guys crashing the popular girls' parties, but we'd kind of make sure they'd know where the party was. The guys would hang out at one end of the room, and the girls would just about elbow each other to cross over and serve them. It sounds so weird now—all of us little harem girls running back and forth with cupcakes, working so hard to be the nicest and most accommodating.

One time Scott looked at what I gave him

and said, "No. Get me chocolate icing," and I guess I was feeling crabby, because I said, "Get it yourself." "A feisty one, huh?" he said, and I said something dumb like "Who was your slave *last* year?" We started talking, kind of mock-insulting each other, and that's when he first noticed me. That's when I learned guys like girls who are challenging. Well, not *too* challenging, just—feisty. So I wasn't going to moan and cry in front of Scott. But . . .

I blurted out the words before I could stop myself. I couldn't hold them in. "If I asked you to stay on the Island, would you?"

His expression was wary. "Are you asking me to turn down Dartmouth?"

"No, I wouldn't do that. I said *if*. *If* I asked you. I just want to know."

"Anything good that happens for me is for the both of us, L.J. In the long run."

"That's not an answer."

"So what kind of question was that? If, if. If the queen had balls, she'd be king."

He was right. It was a dumb question. We turned into the school grounds.

"L.J.?"

"What?"

"Are you mad?"

"No . . . it's just—Scott, I love you so much."

CARA

I'M IN THE SHOWER AND MOMMY IS KNOCKING on the door. I hate when she does that.

"Come on, honey. You've got to get going."

I'm all soapy. I like my skin when it's slippery and bubbly.

"Cara? Time to get out."

"Don't tell me! I know for myself when it's time!"

I don't want to go to school today. Thinking about the test makes my stomach feel funny, and then I don't even want to slide the soap around anymore.

"Cara," Mommy calls, "hurry up!"

I wrap the towel around me and I go to my room. "Mommy?" My hair is wet on my forehead where the shower cap didn't cover it. "What if I can't find a common denominator? What then?"

"Honey, you did it fine last night. If you

multiply the other denominators by each other, you get a common denominator. You can always reduce the fraction later."

All those things are too hard. "But what if—" I twist around to hook the back of my bra.

"You learned it last year. You know it really well."

"But what if I forget?"

"I know you studied hard," Mommy says. "How about some toast?"

My stomach feels bad. "No."

"Just settle down, honey. A little orange juice or—?"

And then I see the new blouse on my bed, folded next to my socks and underpants and denim skirt. "*Oooh*, I love it!" It's pink. Mommy tied a matching ribbon for me, all ready to put in my hair.

Mommy is buttoning up the back. "Stop bouncing, Cara."

"What do you think, does it look beautiful on me?"

"Very nice."

"I love the color! I love everything pink!"

"It's more rose than pink. An unusual color, really," Mommy says. "See that bit of lace around the collar? I couldn't resist it."

"Can I get nail polish to match? Can I?"

Mommy combs and brushes my hair. I smile at myself in the mirror. My hair is long and blond. Mommy rinses it with lemon juice to make it shine. I'm lots prettier than Anne Pierce or Valerie Gold or even Laura Jean Kettering.

When I leave for school, Mommy says, "Don't worry, pussycat. I know you're trying your very best and I'm proud of you."

I wish she'd stop saying things like that. I slam the door. Damn-shit-screw the test! I don't care! My stomach feels bad again.

LAURA JEAN

I could tell right away that Scott and I weren't late; there were still crowds of people hanging out on the front steps of the school.

"Yo, Delaney!" and a punch on his arm from John Masci. "Way to go!" from Bob Dietrich. Joe Lopez was there, too. Everyone had heard; news always travels fast in Shorehaven.

"How's it going, Laura Jean?" Masci was looking at me, sympathetically, I thought. Some people said he was a loudmouth, and he could be a real jerk when he was drunk, but he was always nice to me.

"I think it's great." I gave him a big smile.

Other people came over. We were the biggest group, spreading out over the stairs.

"Hey, fag, nice pants," Masci yelled out at someone. "Where's the flood?"

The boy didn't turn around or answer back; he just scurried by us like he hadn't heard anything.

Scott took my arm. "Come on, I want to tell Gregory."

I followed his glance to Dan Gregory at the top of the stairs, looking down at the parking lot through his camcorder. He hung out with the artsy group and, as far as I could tell, he and Scott had nothing in common. He wasn't one of us. I guess there was a holdover from living next door and playing together all those years when they were little kids, way before I ever knew Scott.

By the time we got there, Mike Clay was standing in front of Dan.

Clay had his arms crossed in front of his chest. "You can't film that."

"What?" Dan impatiently looked up from the viewfinder. "The light's right and—"

"You can't take it."

"Why? The sun is—"

"Because I'm in your way," Clay said.

Dan looked uncomfortable. No one in their right mind tangled with Mike Clay; he was all built-up muscle, with huge shoulders that made him look like a pinhead. Scott said he was a great defensive end.

"Hey, Clay!" Scott landed a playful punch on Mike Clay's shoulder. And to Dan, "What's happening?"

"Nothing. Same old shit," Dan said.

"My mom heard you got into NYU Film."

"Yeah, last week." A smile spread over Dan's face.

"All right!" Scott gave him the high five.

"You want to be a movie director?" I asked, just for something to say.

Mike Clay was almost on top of the camcorder. "So put me in your video."

"Your ugly mug's gonna break the guy's camera," Scott said, laughing. "Leave him alone."

Clay hesitated, then said, "You coming in, Delaney?"

"In a minute . . ."

"OK, see you later."

Dan looked after him. "What's his problem?"

"Clay's all right," Scott said.

"He's an asshole," Dan said.

"Hey—he's OK."

I knew just what Scott was thinking. *We* can say that about Mike Clay, but not an outsider. Scott looked annoyed for only a split second; he's real easy-going and never gets mad unless he's badly provoked.

He was smiling again. "You know what? Dartmouth came through!"

"Yeah, I heard; your mom told mine. That's terrific."

I could picture Mrs. D telling all the neighbors, just going on and on. She boasted too much about her kids, but that wasn't a fault; it was because she was a great mom, always behind Scott, Tommy, and Ginny one hundred percent.

"Yeah, fastest slapshot in the East," Scott said, mocking himself. I had a feeling I'd be hearing that for the rest of the year.

"That's great. I mean it," Dan said.

"So what are you taking pictures of, anyway?" Scott said. "You've always got that thing with you."

"Just—the high school and stuff."

"What's so interesting about Shorehaven?"

"It's not Shorehaven specifically. It's the high school scene—like a documentary, from the inside. Look at the burn-outs meeting under the tree—I could show them there all day long. My problem is showing the passage of time. I guess I could say 'Eight A.M., beginning of the school day.' "

This kid could talk a blue streak about things no one cared about. I shifted my weight.

"Narration's a cheap way out," he went on, "but what the hell. I could catch the same guys there and say 'ten-fifteen—third period,' 'eleven-thirty—fourth period,' show the tree shadows lengthening . . ."

"But you'd have to run in and out of the building all day long," Scott said.

"I know, that's a problem."

A bunch of the girls were clustered on the stairs below us. I could hear someone squealing, "You won't believe what happened!" I wondered what that was about—listen, I like good gossip as much as anybody.

"You could tape 'The Munchkin' making a speech," Scott said. "For comic relief." That's what they called the principal, Mr. Gilmartin.

"Yeah, right," Dan said. "Now look over there; that's great, a Jaguar and an on-its-last-wheels junker parked side by side. I could tell the whole story of this place in visuals."

"This place is beat," Scott said. "Boring as hell. No school spirit, no race riots, nothing."

"You want *race riots?*" Dan gave him a look.

"No." Scott laughed. "Just something for a little excitement. Baseball season's too slow . . . Another month, man, and I'm outta here!"

He doesn't mean it, he's not in a rush to leave, I thought. *It's just talk.*

"I finally got that social studies report done last night," Dan said.

"The Hiroshima thing? No kidding? Was it due today?" Scott said.

Dan nodded.

"I forgot all about it."

"You *forgot* about it?" Dan said incredulously. "It's half of this quarter's grade."

"So what? I'm in Dartmouth, right?"

"If you graduate, big shot," I said.

"I'll graduate, no sweat." Scott laughed and pulled me to him, my neck tucked in the crook of his elbow. He smelled of soap and peppermint gum. "L.J.'s my conscience, my guardian angel."

"No, really," I said. "You better do *something*."

"All right, all right, I'll go in and find something. Come on, L.J."

We walked into school with our arms around each other.

JOE LOPEZ

We were at the hall lockers: me, Mike Clay, Charlie Goren, the Delaneys, Dietrich, and Masci.

"How about cleaning up your shit sometime?" I told Masci. I was looking for my aeronautics notebook in the locker I shared with him; I was getting a shot at the flight trainer today. It was the best class in this freaking school. The teacher knew I was serious; he knew I wanted to join the Air Force after graduation.

I found the notebook under a pile of Masci's garbage. *¡Ay, ese cochino!* "What the hell is this?" I held up a stained T-shirt between my thumb and forefinger. "It stinks."

"Yeah, it's corroded," Masci said cheerfully.

Scott said, "He's gonna contaminate you, Lopez."

We started fooling around about the different diseases Masci could be carrying: the clap, AIDS, herpes . . .

"Masci'll screw anything that moves."

"Yeah, he's been dipping in some funny pools."

Masci shoved Tommy, laughing. "At least I'm gettin' some."

So it was turning kind of rowdy when Yvonne Garcia and Eliana Castro came walking by us.

I froze. I knew the guys would say something. I knew it.

The girls were wearing lace tops and tight skirts with sparkling too-wide belts. They teetered past us on high heels, talking to each other a mile a minute in Spanish. Yvonne had a gold heart locket bouncing against her boobs.

Masci started making loud kissing noises, smacking his lips, and Scott called, "Shake your *cucaracha!*" Mike Clay laughed.

Eliana looked back over her shoulder, straight at me. I had to look away fast. She was from El Salvador, like me, except I've been here a lot longer.

"Check out that ass on her," Charlie Goren said, loud enough for the girls to hear.

I wished he'd shut the hell up. I *knew* Eliana. Why did they have to be so off-the-boat dumb and look like a couple of *putas!* I knew why: They were dressed up, wanting to look pretty for school. To them, Polos and Reeboks were too plain and unfeminine. To tell the truth, I could see that myself, but hell, couldn't they look around and do like the Americans?

It was like that time Luis Melendez got in trouble. The whole time Mr. Metzer was yelling at him and accusing him of things, Luis kept his eyes down, anyplace away from Metzer's. I could tell Metzer was going to give Luis real shit, thinking he was shifty-eyed and guilty. Gringo teachers didn't understand about showing respect for authority by not looking right at them. Poor dumb Luis, with his Latino good manners.

"Sluts," Scott said.

The girls were at the end of the hall.

Goren nudged me. "Hey, José, go for it."

My face got hot; I was glad my skin was dark enough so it wouldn't show, not like Tommy's, who got ragged all the time for blushing. Goren was kidding around, the way he'd call Bluestein "Jew-stein," teammates kidding around, ranking each other, but— My real name is Julio, Julio Lopez; everyone calls me Joe. Even Mama finally got used to taking phone calls for "Joe." I hated that José crap. (Mama had a good blouse a lot like Eliana's.)

I knew for a fact that Eliana's father was old-fashioned strict. She couldn't even go out with a guy by herself. The truth was Latino girls were more careful with themselves, more careful than the *Americanas* with their squeaky-clean blond hair and clear blue eyes and curses coming out of their perfect mouths like they knew they could get away with anything. The *Americanas* fooled around plenty.

Sometimes I almost hated the guys, but they were my buddies for real now. It had been a couple of years since I'd crossed over from Latin League soccer to football, because football meant something in Shorehaven. I wasn't as hot as Dietrich, but I was damn good. I more than held my own. I was one of the "in" guys, hung out with them, partied with them. I was somebody around the school. Everyone knew Joe Lopez was all right.

"Wake up and smell the coffee," Masci was saying.

"What?"

"You coming or not?" The third period bell was ringing.

"Yeah, yeah, I'm coming," I said.

The seven of us, seven together dudes, went down the crowded hall and a path cleared for us.

Mike Clay was still talking about Eliana and Yvonne, laughing about getting a bite of hot and spicy dark meat. I wanted to punch his face in. I'd show them! One of these days, I'd hump the ears off some blond WASP bitch!

LAURA JEAN

THIRD PERIOD, ANIMAL SCIENCE, WAS ENDLESS. John Masci and Bob Dietrich were in the class, too. Masci was sprawled out on his desk, half asleep. Bob, on the other side of the room, sat up straight, busily taking notes. Bob always stands and sits like he's got a pole stuck up his back.

Mr. Held was scratching something about vertebrates on the blackboard. A long list of different bones.

I looked at the wall clock. It seemed like the minute hand never moved. I looked out the window; all I could see was the parking lot and a bit of the field. I looked at the snake that Mr. Held kept in a cage on the shelf. It was coiled, not doing anything. I wondered if it felt cooped up.

"Tibia," Mr. Held said. "The inner of the two bones of the vertebrate hind limb between the knee and the ankle."

I started writing in my notebook, but I wound up doodling. "L.J. 'n' S 4-Ever." "Laura Jean Kettering" and "Laura Jean Delaney" in bubble letters. Almost everyone calls me Laura Jean, but Scott shortened it to L.J. and a lot of people picked that up from him. Scott's shortened it even more to his private name for me: Elly. I don't think anyone knows about that. He calls me Elly when he's thinking about making love.

"Come on, Elly, come on . . ."

We started going out in seventh grade. Back then, kids were going out and breaking up every three weeks, playing pretend with love. By six months we'd set some kind of record. And then it was ten months, a year, on through eighth grade . . . Not that it was always smooth going. We were still such kids. Our almost-breaking-up fight was so stupid.

Scott and I had gone from being self-conscious with each other to talking about all kinds of things. But when he was with the other eighth-grade boys, he acted different. Like when we were going somewhere, he'd walk in front with the other boys and leave me to walk behind him with the girls. Well, one time we were going to the movies after school; a bunch of us were walking down Main Street, Scott ahead with the boys and me trotting behind with Monica and Pat. But Monica and Pat stopped off at the drugstore, and I found myself alone and three paces behind him. I felt dumb and it made me mad.

"Scott!" I yelled. I had to yell for him to hear me. "Scott!"

He finally stopped and turned around. "What?"

"I'm not your squaw!"

"What's your problem?"

He got mad because I was telling him what to do in front of the boys; I wound up turning around and going home, and Scott was too stubborn to come after me. We didn't talk to each other for almost a week. And then Scott came over to my house one night and said, "Do you want to break up?" and I said, "I thought we did." He said, "But do you *want* to?" and I said, "Do you?" and he said, "I asked first," and I said, "Well, do you?" and then he said, "No," and I was so relieved.

We were only fifteen when we finally did it. It was the first time for both of us. "I don't even know if I'm doing this right," he said to me that very first time, and somehow we got through the nervousness, through the awkwardness of a condom and gobs of foam. Scott had heard someplace that Saran Wrap would be enough, but that didn't sound right to me, and I wasn't taking any chances.

We're both Catholic and doing something against the rules together drew us closer and maybe made it more exciting in a way. I stopped going to confession then, because I knew I'd keep right on. I felt terrible about not being able to take Communion anymore, and that's when I stopped going to church altogether. Scott kept on taking Communion, and the way he worked that out never made any sense to me. I couldn't compromise.

The year I was eleven, I read about the lives of the saints. I imagined myself with baby fat melted away, pared down to the bone, burning with passion, strong and brave and true as Joan of Arc. I gave up just about everything for Lent that year—to make it hard, to test myself, and to see if I measured up. Dad said if hair shirts were available in Shorehaven, I'd be wearing one. I thought a lot about becoming a nun— not to be sheltered in a convent but to wash the feet of the diseased and destitute. I wanted to lose myself in great sacrifices. "It's a phase, it'll pass," Mom said. "You wanted to be a veterinarian last year." I knew she was laughing at me, and at that moment, I hated her.

The only one who understood was my best friend, Pat. She had a passion, too, though hers was only for horses. She'd travel all the way into the city to bring lumps of sugar to the horses that pull hansom cabs at Central Park. That year, Pat never walked or ran; she trotted or cantered. Of course, I was the only one who knew. The riding lessons her folks finally gave her didn't satisfy her. She wanted to ride bareback, on a wild, free horse—becoming one—her hair and its mane streaming together in the wind. Pat had short hair, but I knew what she meant.

The first year of junior high, Pat and I got our periods within a month of each other. She was thrilled at officially becoming a woman. When my time came, I cried. It sounds silly now, but I still remember the feeling of loss. I suppose I sensed, on the brink of my teens, that I wouldn't renounce the flesh.

I gave up my saints. Sometimes I think that dumb kid was the best and truest part of me. But God is everywhere, not just in church, and loving Scott made me kinder and more unselfish.

At the beginning Scott was more into it than I was; he wanted it all the time and sometimes I felt sore, but I never said anything. Then it changed and it was like I wanted it even more than he did. Or wanted it more with *him* than he did with *me*. I think that's what our breakup was about, and that time it wasn't a stupid little thing—it was serious.

It was just last year and it came right out of the blue. We'd been together all this time, and one night Scott and I were talking and he said, "Maybe it's a good idea for us to take a breather."

"What do you mean?"

"You know, see other people for a while."

I was so stunned. All I could say was, "Why?"

"I was thinking, I've never gone out with anyone else . . . That's weird when you think about it."

"I thought we were in love," I said. "I thought we loved each other."

"Well, yeah, I love you, L.J., but—like we've been tied up since, holy shit, since seventh grade! I don't mean break up *forever*, but I just want to . . ."

"You want to what?" I was numb.

"It's different for a guy," he said. "Guys get curious, that's all. It doesn't mean we can't stay friends, but I want to see what it's like with—"

"Do what you want," I said. "With anyone you want. Any skank you want! But don't think we'll be friends!"

It might have been easier if I didn't have to see him around school all the time. We didn't talk, but I was still in the same group; it was bad enough without retreating to Siberia and cutting myself off completely. I tried to act like I didn't care. I'd be in the middle of the crowd, joking around and laughing, and everything I did and said was fake. I lost ten pounds that month. I'm not sorry about that, but I lost it all at once, without even trying.

I remember John Masci from that terrible time. I was standing with him one day when Scott walked by with his arm around Melinda Godfrey. Masci said, "You know what I think, L.J.? I think he's out of his freakin' mind." So when people say Masci's crude, I always remember that.

Now Held was scratching a diagram on the board. Some of the kids were copying it. The digestive system of invertebrates.

"This will be on the test," Mr. Held was saying.

My page was nothing but doodles. I'd have to get the notes from Bob Dietrich later; he has the neatest handwriting. Masci and Dietrich took animal science because everyone knew Held was an easy marker. I thought I'd like it, but I don't.

I don't know if it's me or because Mr. Held makes it so boring. Once I'd thought I wanted to be a veterinarian. That was back in elementary school; I have a cat, Muffin, and I'd take her to the vet for shots and ear mites. The vet was a lady, and I liked the way she took charge of Muffin and knew exactly what she was doing. She'd explain things to me and she was so smart; I wanted to be just like her.

"This will be on the test," Mr. Held said, "and Chapter Thirteen."

"Aw, c'mon," Masci called out. "Just give us the answers, man."

Mr. Held grinned stupidly.

Held was an ass. He read *Soldier of Fortune* magazine and he tried too hard to be cool. He bent over backward for the popular kids: the jocks and jockettes. I couldn't respect that, but so what, I needed all the help I could get. Well, so much for Laura Jean, Veterinarian. Anyway, I'd grown up. I was more interested in becoming Laura Jean Delaney. Maybe I'd have some kind of glamour job in the city and we'd be like a yuppie couple and I'd have Scott's babies . . .

The terrible time ended about a month later. Scott came over to me at one of the keg parties.

"Come on, we have to talk," he said, pulling me away from a group of the girls.

"What?" I said. "I have nothing to say to you."

"Listen, I want to go out again."

"What?"

"I miss you, L.J. Splitting was the dumbest thing we ever did. I miss you."

"Just like that?" I said.

Scott was smiling, that crooked smile he has when he wants to charm someone. "I really love you, L.J."

I punched him hard in the chest. It took him completely by surprise; the smile faded.

"You can't do that! You change your mind and snap, it's OK? Like it was nothing? Like it was nothing?"

Maybe I'd had too much beer or maybe something gave. "You can't do that to me!" I kept repeating, punching and punching. Scott stood rigid, his arms at his sides, taking it, looking miserable. "You can't do that to me! You can't put me through hell and think I'll still be there!"

I was making a scene. Through a blur, I saw the other kids around us, watching. Scott stood still, looking miserable and embarrassed. "You're right," he said.

He didn't make a move to defend himself or ward me off.

"I know," he said. "You're right."

I hit him and hit him, and my voice got hoarse and then I started coughing. It was like the tears I wouldn't cry got stuck in my throat, and I was coughing so hard I was gasping for breath and I thought I'd choke. I couldn't stop coughing for anything.

Scott patted my back. "You OK, L.J.?"

I shook my head no, and he put his arms around me and held me tight.

"I'm sorry," he whispered. "Elly, who else is gonna feed you peeled raisins one by one? Who loves ya, baby?"

That breather proved to me that life without Scott is a black hole. And it proved to Scott that he *really* loved me.

"A lot of girls act sweet, but they're playing a role," he said. "There's no one like you, L.J. No one else is so sweet."

Me, sweet? I knew I was too impatient and had an evil temper. Mom was always saying, "You can get more with honey than with vinegar, Laura Jean."

I didn't know how I was supposed to be feisty and sweet at the same time, but I tried hard to be nicer. We were closer than ever after the break. The only thing is, I'd never noticed the restlessness in Scott before that. It scared me.

"Hey, there's no law against *looking,* is there?" he'd say.

The bell finally rang and we filed out of the classroom.

I passed by the snake. Everyone thinks snakes are slimy, but they're really not; their skin is dry. Mr. Held usually fed the snake during his fourth period class. He said sometime he'd feed it for ours. All the girls said, "*Ooooh,* gross," but I thought it would be interesting. I even did my own labs, though most of the popular girls got the guys to do them. But I'm not squeamish.

I wished animal science was more about real animals and not mostly memorizing the names of bones.

CARA

THERE'S NO TRACK PRACTICE THIS AFTERNOON, so I came straight home from school. I get tired of practicing, but I like running in the meets. Mrs. Jensen says I get good times. When they say my name over the P.A. in school the next day, I feel proud. I like Mrs. Jensen, except when she said, "Pay attention, Cara, stop dreaming! You have to be ready for your events; I can't always keep tabs on you." She only said it that one time. She's nice.

Track is my favorite thing in school, and lunch on Tuesdays and Thursdays. That's when I have the same lunch period as Anne Pierce. I sit with her. She lives across the street and we walk home from track practice together. On Tuesdays and Thursdays, I have lunch with her and her friends. Even though they're busy talking with each other, I like to sit with them. The cafeteria is too noisy and crowded. When I have no one to sit with, I buy a sandwich and eat it outside or in the girls' room. I won't sit at a table with the other special education kids because some of them look funny.

Mommy is painting this afternoon. I like the way paint smells. She writes beautiful picture books. She does the words and the pictures all by herself. Her books are in the public library and in the elementary school library. She wrote lots of other picture books, too, but the Bunnies are the best ones. Mommy says we can stay in this house, even though Daddy left, because of the Bunnies. Sometimes she fights with Daddy on the phone and says the check is late and where is the check.

There's Mother Bunny and Baby Bunny; the baby hops away and has adventures, but the mother always finds her at the end and brings her home to the hollow tree, safe and sound. There is *Bunnies on Parade*, *Bunny and the Circus Pony*, *Bunny's Picnic*, *Bunny Meets the Fox*, and the almost finished one is *Bunny's Great Adventure*.

Mommy works hard and I help her. In *Bunny's Great Adventure*, where Mother Bunny rescues Baby Bunny from the hawk, Mother Bunny was screaming and trying to cover Baby with her own body, and there was a terrible thumping of her heart and her eyes were wide open and wild, and the hawk's big shadow was right over her and took up the whole page. It made me feel bad. It was too scary. I told Mommy, and she looked it over and she said, "You're right, Cara. I don't know what I was thinking of. You're absolutely right." She fixed the painting and she typed new words in her computer.

I learn how to type in school. The teacher said I can type twenty words a minute, and I told Mommy. She said that was so good and she got all excited about teaching me on her computer. Every time I did something wrong, the computer went *beep*. I didn't want to, but she said at least try. *Beep*. "It's no different from a typewriter, you just have to"—there were too many things. *Beep, beep, beep*—I got so mad. I yelled "I don't care!" and threw the keyboard against the wall. She didn't make me do it anymore.

Mommy likes it when I help her with the Bunnies. She hugs me and says I'm her best editor. Editors are very important.

"What would I ever do without you?" Mommy says.

LAURA JEAN

I WENT TO THE SENIOR SPORTS AWARDS DINNER with Scott's family. Baseball and track weren't completely finished yet, but they held the Sports Awards Dinner early to keep it special and separate from the rush of other things that happened around graduation—finals and Regents, the teacher recognition tea, the scholastic and arts awards, the Fling . . . They give out the other awards in a long, boring assembly in the auditorium between classes; the athletes were the only ones who got a special dinner.

It seemed like everything was winding to an end. I'd seen the kids working on the yearbook the day before and it made me sad; they were manufacturing memories before our time was even over. In the yearbook, they had put Bob Dietrich as the most handsome and Charlie Goren for the most popular.

The Booster Club parents—the Delaneys

were very active in that—had done a fantastic job on the cafeteria. Tables for ten were set up all around the room. The decorations were red, white, and blue: red tulips, blue hydrangea, and miniature American flags on white tablecloths. It looked so pretty. It even smelled different; there were traces of perfume and after-shave instead of the usual hamburger grease.

I sat between Scott and Bob. Tommy and Ginny sat between Mr. and Mrs. Delaney. Next to Bob, there were two empty chairs saved for his parents. The boys looked different and older in suits and starched white shirts. I couldn't wait to get out of my dress and high heels; I'd left jeans at Scott's to change into for the party at Charlie Goren's later.

The cloth was scattered with crumbs of chocolate cake. I sipped my coffee.

"Think I can slip out for a quick smoke?" Mr. Delaney said.

Mrs. Delaney patted her lips with a napkin. "No, look, they're about to start." She leaned across the empty chairs and squeezed Bob's hand. "I'm sure they'll be here any minute."

"I thought you were quitting, Mr. D," I said.

"I have quit. At least four or five times."

I smiled. That was his running joke.

"Here comes The Munchkin," Scott said.

Mr. Gilmartin was at the dais, tapping the mike. "Parents, athletes, and friends . . . It is with great pride that I . . ."

It was going to take forever to wade through all the speeches.

". . . and this evening, we salute your service to Shorehaven High School . . ."

Tony Edison was sitting in the front. He's on the local evening news on TV. I'd seen him around town before. He lives in Ocean Point and does a lot of fund-raising things—but it's still odd to see someone who's so familiar to you from TV. I wondered if he was going to speak or what.

". . . an outstanding year . . . the cream of the crop . . . crowned by the Shorehaven Kings, our Nassau County Conference A champions . . ."

Gilmartin was talking about the football team, and I recognized Mike Clay's piercing whistle and Masci's bark from across the room.

". . . on the playing fields of Shorehaven . . . continued success in all your endeavors."

It was time for the awards. Coach after coach stood up to speak. Track, swim team, lacrosse, on and on.

I studied the flowers—the tulips were drooping; I watched Ginny fidgeting. Scott looked sharp tonight. He caught my eye and whispered, "I like that dress." He sometimes said things as though he'd just read my mind. That happened a lot lately.

". . . most valuable player in girls' field hockey is—Jeanette Trilby!"

There was scattered applause as a butch girl trotted to the dais to get her trophy.

". . . for boys' basketball, the man with the spirit and the heart, the most valuable player, the one and only 'Spike' Washington!"

Loud cheers and stomping from the two black tables. Funny how Shorehaven football was all white. I guess high school kids wanted to play with the same people they hung out with. Like the tennis team was almost all Jews and the soccer team had a lot of Latinos. Well, football was kind of mixed—Lopez was Dominican or Colombian or something like that, and there was Bluestein.

". . . and that's why wrestling's most valuable player is—John Masci!"

"Way to go, Masci!" Scott yelled.

"Way to go!" Tommy echoed.

There were lots of cheers from all around the

room, because John Masci was in our group. It would be like that at graduation, too. You could tell someone's popularity by the amount of applause when their name was called for the diploma.

I'd heard that at graduation last year, when Noreen Malivek went up for her diploma, all the senior boys stood up and gave her a standing ovation—because Noreen had laid most of them. It was really gross.

"We've got it sewed up tonight," Scott said.

"I guess," Bob said.

"I'm getting hockey, you're getting football, I bet Goren gets baseball . . ."

"Dad said he'd try to get away early; it's hard for him, though, you know, if he gets tied up at a meeting." The muscle in Bob's cheek twitched.

"Don't be so sure of yourself, Scott," Ginny piped up. "Someone else could get it." She was OK, just doing some kid-sister needling.

"Why don't you shut up," from Scott.

"Well, they could. I'm just saying . . ."

"*Ssshhh*, here we go," Mr. Delaney said as the hockey coach rose.

"We've had a great season and a truly outstanding team this year. The spark plug, the guy who always came through, the recipient of a well-deserved full hockey scholarship to Dartmouth, our most valuable player, is none other than—Scott Delaney!"

Our table went wild, and I could feel my heart swell. Scott strolled up to the dais, cool as a cucumber—I loved the way he did everything so nonchalant—but I knew he was excited. Mrs. D's face was shining. Scott shook hands with the coach and held the trophy high on his way back to the table. Mr. Delaney, beaming, got up and hugged him. Mrs. Delaney kissed him noisily on the cheek. Ginny was bouncing and clapping, Bob slapped his shoulder, and then I was caught up in his hug.

"I'm so proud of you," I said. "I'm *so* proud of you."

". . . and baseball's most valuable player is that man with the golden arm, our never-say-die pitcher—Tim Hughes."

"Shit, I thought Goren would get it," Scott said.

"Tim's OK," Bob said.

Football came last. The most important thing always came last. And when Coach Barrett rose to speak, the room became still. You could have heard a pin drop.

There was something about Coach Barrett.

The boys kidded around with him and everything, but they looked up to him. Even Clay watched his language around him.

"The thing about Coach Barrett," Scott once told me, "is he cares about you for yourself. Cochran, he likes me as long as I'm hot on ice, but if your skills fall off, he doesn't know you. Barrett's different."

It was true. He invited the boys over to barbecues at his house, and last year when Mike Clay's mother was dying of cancer, Scott said he'd spent a lot of extra time with Mike. I wondered if he and his wife couldn't have children of their own. He would have made a great father.

He was one-hundred-percent man, Scott had said, but he was spiritual, too. Before every game, he had them stand in a circle, holding hands, and led a prayer.

"Do you pray to win?" I'd asked.

"No. We pray to support our teammates, one for all and all for one, and to do our best. It's kind of general, 'cause there's Protestants and Bluestein."

"Do you all say it with him?"

"No. We hold hands and when he's through, we have like a silent prayer."

I was curious. "What's your silent prayer? I mean, in a locker room?"

"Me? I mainly think, and feel the fellowship." Scott had grinned. "Coach's word."

It made me a little jealous, though I knew that was silly. There was something powerful in the locker room, and I was left out of it.

"Ladies and gentlemen, I'm pleased to present the football award tonight. I've been privileged to work with an outstanding group of young men . . ."

Coach Barrett stood tall and erect; he was kind of old, but he was in great shape.

"I believe in the Greek ideal of a sound mind in a sound body—" He paused and laughed. "Stop me if you've heard that before."

Scott, Tommy, and Bob nodded and smiled.

"—and I'm proud to say my boys strive to be their best, mentally and physically, both on and off the field. Their victories have been victories of courage and stamina and teamwork, and they'll take those values with them wherever life leads. I know they'll do us proud.

"To the graduating seniors—Mike Clay, Joe Lopez, John Masci, Jack Bluestein, Charlie Goren, Scott Delaney, Bob Dietrich—you've been an inspiration for the guys coming up. The

Shorehaven Kings were a *team*, a great team—
I love you guys—but the most valuable player
award has to single out one extraordinary indi-
vidual, one of the most talented athletes I've
ever coached. In every way, he pushes himself
to the limit and strives for excellence—and
Bobby, we'll watch you excel in Boston next
year. The most valuable player, Bob Dietrich!"

The applause that had started with the first
mention of his name swelled to a roar. The coach
put his arm around Bob's shoulders as he gave
him the trophy. Then Tony Edison joined them
at the dais. His hair was very dark and shiny,
just like on TV.

"I think Coach Barrett has said it all," Edison
said. "I'd like to add that, as a fellow resident,
I take great pride in Shorehaven's excellence.
I'm pleased to announce that the *Long Island
Press* pick for this year's high school football
MVP is—Bob Dietrich!" He smiled at Bob's
flushed surprise and handed him a certificate.
"Congratulations."

When Bob returned to the table, Mr. and Mrs.
Delaney hugged him and acted exactly as excited
as they had for Scott.

"That's wonderful, Bob, wonderful! Imagine,
the *Long Island Press!*"

"We've got a bunch of winners here—what a bunch of super kids!"

They were just great, really warm—that's why not only Bob, but everybody, hung out at the Delaneys so much.

"I can't believe his folks didn't show," I whispered to Scott.

Bob gave no sign that anyone was missing; he was always in perfect control. But then, just as the evening was breaking up, the Dietrichs came rushing in. I would have been mad as a wet hen, but Bob looked happy that they'd made it. Then everyone was telling them about the award and about the *Long Island Press*, Mrs. Delaney bubbling about it, and all Mr. Dietrich did was shake Bob's hand and say, "Well done, son."

Bob seemed so overjoyed at that . . . I had to look away.

We had the best time after the dinner. The party at Charlie Goren's was fun, but the real best time was later.

At Charlie's, it was like after a football victory—everyone in a good mood, the boys full of themselves and making a lot of noise. There was a lot of touching extended index fingers and yelling "Number one! Shorehaven Kings! Number one!" At one point, they even started the between-halves locker-room chant that they do: the bunch of them in a semicircle, chanting, "We've got it! They want it! We're keepin' it!" over and over, clapping out the beat.

There was a keg, of course, and somebody brought a bottle of champagne, and Scott, Clay, and Masci poured it over Dietrich. He got soaking wet and had to change into one of Goren's shirts, but he knew they did it because it was truly his night. If Goren minded being passed over for the baseball award, it didn't show; he's a great guy. He said, "Hey, how about that Scott Delaney!" and everyone was going, "Yay, Scott!"

Goren has a great sound system. We were dancing to everything from Rolling Stones to Hammer. Joe Lopez can *move*. I watched him for a while, thinking he's very sexy. None of my girlfriends ever went out with a Hispanic. John Masci is just as dark as Lopez but he's Italian, and I guess that makes it different.

When "We Are Family" came on, everybody was up and dancing, and we all sang along at the top of our lungs, yelling out "fam-i-ly!" It's great to be with real friends, friends close as any family.

After the party broke up, Scott and I, Bob

and Annette, and Masci and Tina—just us three couples—went over to the Delaneys'. Of course, Tommy came home, too, but I guess he was tired because he went upstairs pretty soon. We were lounging on the sofas in the Delaneys' family room, feeling mellow. They're the most comfortable sofas—you sink in and you never want to get up again. I like Tina a lot; she's been dating Masci for just a little while and she's a sophomore, but she's a real pisser. Annette looked bored. Scott calls her The Ice Queen. She's not one of us; she's only been with Bob for a few weeks. They seem kind of strained together; I had the feeling he was dating her just because everyone says she's the most beautiful girl in school, and she was with him just because he was Bob Dietrich. I didn't think they'd last long.

Anyway, we were sitting around talking, our voices low because Mr. and Mrs. Delaney and Ginny were asleep upstairs. Tina said, "Let's have a fire," so we turned on the air conditioner and made a fire in the fireplace. The only light was from the flames, and it was so romantic. Scott put on some of his dad's old records. Mr. D has a collection of old stuff, a lot of Sinatra and people I've never even heard of. We kid him about those dumb old songs—everything is "moon, June, croon." But then Scott made a point of putting on a particular record and said, "Dance with me."

The music swelled up, a little scratchy because it was so ancient.

Scott looked at me with the warmest smile. "The girl that I marry," he said.

"What?" I said breathlessly.

" 'The Girl That I Marry.' " He laughed. "The name of the song. By Irving Berlin."

"Oh," I said. I felt embarrassed about misunderstanding. But his next words made it all right.

"It fits the girl in my arms to a T," he whispered.

Neither of us is any good at slow dancing; we just held on, real close, and swayed to the music. And Scott was singing along with the lyrics. He didn't know them that well, he skipped some and kind of stumbled through. Something about her being as soft and as sweet as a nursery.

I felt his breath against my cheek.

She'd have polished nails and wear satin and lace and flowers in her hair. She'd be like a little kitten purring. Like a doll. Anyway, that was what he was whisper-singing in my ear, telling me I was that girl he wanted to marry.

"You're the one, L.J.," he said.

I was seeing myself through his eyes, a baby-pure virginal ideal. I *was* like a virgin, in a way; I'd never been with anyone but Scott and he knew that. It was important to him. I swore to myself that I'd never curse again—though he did, he hated it coming out of my mouth. I'd always be soft and sweet and feminine. We were close in the firelight and I felt so moved.

"Let's go to my room," he whispered. "I have a present for you."

I was getting too soppy sentimental, so I said, "Right. God's gift to women."

"No, a real present," he said.

In his room he handed me a wrapped box, and I said, "It's not my birthday or anything . . ."

"Just because I want to. Well, I was going to save it for after the Fling but—"

I ripped the paper, all thumbs, and there was a jeweler's box. Inside, a gold chain bracelet with a big heart charm.

"Oh, Scott! Tonight was *your* night, I should have gotten *you* something!"

"Read what it says." He was grinning at me, watching for my reaction, looking so boyish and adorable.

L.J. AND SCOTT was engraved on the heart.

"Turn it over, read the other side."

It said ETERNAL LOVE.

I threw my arms around his neck. "Oh, Scott, I love love *love* you!"

I felt like the luckiest girl. I felt so blessed.

CARA

I'M WALKING HOME FROM TRACK PRACTICE WITH Anne Pierce and Valerie. Mostly we cut through the woods next to the field because that's a short-cut. Anne says she wants to go the front way because she's hungry, so we go on the Boulevard and stop at the bakery. Valerie says she'll split a roll with Anne. I don't want anything. They go in the bakery. I wait outside.

I don't like to go in there and smell the bakery smells.

Different people own it now, but I don't like to go in there.

I used to get jelly doughnuts all the time on the way home from school. I loved the ones with strawberry jam the best.

Once, way back when I was in sixth grade, I went in and the lady wasn't there. The man from the back was behind the counter. I asked him for a strawberry jelly doughnut. He said if I came in the back, he'd show me where he bakes them and he'd give me *two*. So I went in the back. He sat down in the chair. He pulled me on his lap.

"Sweet girl," he said.

He held me in his lap. It was like when Daddy used to take me on his lap and read a story to me, before he left us. But the man was sweaty and smelled like B.O., and Daddy didn't smell that way. Then he tickled me down there. It felt bad and scary and good all at the same time. He took his thing out. I didn't want to look, it was red and ugly. He said to kiss it. I shook my head no, but he said, "Do what I tell you." I didn't know what to do; I sat very still on his lap. It was hot back there. He said, "Make believe it's a lollipop." I kept my eyes closed very tight, and I smelled the bread and flour and yeast, and then he gave me two jelly doughnuts. I had flour on my shirt from the man's apron—it was a navy blue shirt—and I brushed it off.

He gave me two jelly doughnuts. I had one to eat and one to save for later in the white paper bakery bag. I licked all the sugar off first, because it's so powdery and I didn't want it to fly all over my clothes. Then I ate all around. I saved the jelly part in the middle for last. Sometimes the jelly's not right in the middle and I bite into it by mistake ahead of time.

Then Mommy saw me with sugar all around my mouth and another doughnut still in the bag. "*Two* of them?" she said, and she laughed. "You've inherited my sweet tooth."

I told her the bakery man gave them to me for free. Mommy was always waiting for Daddy's check.

"That was nice of him," she said. She was still smiling. "I guess you're their best customer."

I said I didn't like it so much because I saw roaches in the back where the ovens are. She stopped smiling, and she asked what I was doing in the back. Then she started asking me a whole lot of other questions. She got upset and mad at everything I said. She scared me. Then she called on the telephone and a policeman came, but he wasn't wearing a uniform, he was wearing a regular suit. He asked me a lot of questions. And the next day, other men came and asked me more questions. I was scared and I started crying, and Mommy was crying, too. I was crying and I begged Mommy, I said, "Please don't make me tell about it anymore," and the man said, "If you want to press charges, she has to—" and Mommy said, "Cara, one more time . . ."

Mommy talked to me about it. She said he was a bad man and my body was my own private property and I didn't have to do everything I was told, even if it was a grown-up. He called me "sweet stuff" and "honey pie," but he smelled bad.

After it was over, I didn't go past the bakery for a long time. I always walked on the other side of the street. Then one day, I passed by. The man wasn't there anymore. There were all new people. But I never go in there.

LAURA JEAN

IT WAS A COUPLE OF DAYS AFTER THE AWARDS. Everyone was congratulating Bob when he came into animal science. Mr. Held said, "Way to go, man!" which sounded phony coming from him. The girls were clustering around Bob, edging each other out to say nice things. Bob's a good guy, but I don't see why the girls make such a fuss over him. Good looks aren't everything. He's kind of stiff and too perfect; he doesn't have that much personality. What really annoys me is when someone tries to get friendly with me just because I'm Scott's girlfriend and they know Scott and Bob are best friends. I can tell when someone's trying to use me, and it makes me mad.

Anyway, the class finally settled down. And then Mr. Held said that it was our turn to see him feed the snake. *After* we went over Chapter Sixteen.

Chapter Sixteen was about enzymes and how they break the food down in carnivores and herbivores. Held droned on and on. Those enzymes would be on the final for sure. I looked over at the snake in its cage on the shelf. If it was hungry because it was eating late today, you couldn't tell. It was coiled, motionless.

I looked around and then I saw the small brown pet box. I recognized it; it was from the pet store on Main Street where I get treats for Muffin. Wait, was the snake going to eat something *live?* And I remembered—of course, snakes eat live prey. Maybe I was imagining it; I thought I saw the box moving a bit. I couldn't keep my eyes off the box. I couldn't concentrate on the chapter.

"OK," Held finally said. "Chow time. Watch this."

For the first time in the period, the class came to attention.

He opened the little box and tipped a white mouse into the cage. At first, it sniffed around cautiously. All I could think was, *It's a pet mouse, the kind they sell for pets!* The snake raised its head, suddenly alert. Then the mouse started to carry on. It squeaked something terrible.

The girls started going "*Eeeow*, gross" and that

egged the boys on to yell "Go, snake!" and "C'mon, get him!" Masci was the worst, cheering and having a great time. Mr. Held was laughing along with them, acting like one of the guys. I couldn't breathe.

The mouse was squealing and squeaking as the snake watched, ready to strike. The mouse ran in circles against the sides of the cage in blind panic. Its body made soft thuds against the glass.

"I can't watch this!" I jumped out of my seat and headed toward the door.

"You girls," Held said, disgusted. "So squeamish." He yanked my arm and pulled me back into the room. "Sit down! Now!"

"I'm not squeamish!" I wouldn't look, but I kept hearing the thuds and the desperate squeals. Masci yelled something and everybody laughed. "This is sick! This is really sick!"

"Oh? You want the poor little snake to starve?" Held minced the words, performing for the class, and they laughed.

"So feed it privately." My voice was shaking.

"You walk and you've got an F for the quarter!"

"I don't care!" I ran out of there, ran from the terrible sounds.

The word got around, of course. Everything

spreads so fast around here. Later, when I came out of math, Scott, Masci, and the crew were coming out of the cafeteria. I went over and they all started going "*Squeak, squeak-squeak, squeak!*"

"Come on, guys," I said, but they wouldn't stop.

"I want to talk," I said to Scott, but Scott was laughing and the squeaking went on. All of them were doing it.

"Cut it out!"

"Oh-oh, Laura Jean's getting mad." Charlie Goren threw his hands up and made a big show of mock fear.

Then Masci was right in my face and squealing.

"You jerk-off. You dumb asshole!" I turned and ran out the front door. I sat down on the steps outside. My whole body was shaking.

Scott followed me out. He was standing over me.

"What?" I said. "You want to squeak some more?"

"What's wrong with you?" he said. "What did you say that to Masci for?"

I shook my head.

"I thought you were a good sport. Since when can't you take a little kidding?"

I was too angry to talk.

"Oh," he said. "You're mad. You're calling my friend names and *you're* mad."

I scraped chipped polish off my thumbnail. Sunlight gleamed off the gold heart on my wrist.

Somebody went up the steps past us.

Scott sat down next to me. "Clay said, 'Your girlfriend must be on the rag.' "

"What did you say?"

"Nothing. What was I supposed to say? You're acting too thin-skinned."

I scraped at my thumbnail.

"It came from a *pet* store," I said. "It couldn't even run; it was trapped . . . Held was encouraging them to *enjoy* it."

"So what did Masci ever do to you?"

"Held made a circus out of it, everyone laughing and— It was the mouse's *life* and there was no respect for— They were laughing at its last— Masci was the worst. He was having a real good time . . . What's the *matter* with everybody?"

"I guess it was a break from the boring stuff."

"You didn't see—" *He wasn't there,* I thought. *If he'd seen it, he'd understand.*

"That mouse was gonna get eaten anyway," Scott said. "Why did you— Snakes have to eat mice. That's the way it is."

"I know that, that's not the point."

"You think your cat is nice to mice? Try her sometime."

"That's different," I said. "Cats are cats."

"Sure they are." Scott was half smiling, trying to make me smile. "Cats are cats. No one's gonna argue with that."

I didn't even know anymore what I was trying to prove.

"Held's a loser," I finally said. "I'm getting an F for the quarter."

"That was a dumb move," Scott said. "What are you, 'The Crusader for Little Creatures'?"

I tried to lighten up. "It's a tough job, but somebody's got to do it." Well, maybe it was dumb, but it was *right*. But Scott wasn't there, he didn't see.

"You can get around him," he said. "Go talk to him. I'll help you think up something. And even if he averages it in, you still pass for the year, don't you?"

"I guess. With a D."

"So what?"

True, I was graduating anyway. It didn't matter.

"I'm late for my class," he said. He stood up, waiting. "L.J.?"

"I'll go inside in a minute," I said. "You go ahead."

He studied my face. "See you later?"

"Sure. Go ahead." Why make a federal case about some stupid teasing?

Sometimes he didn't know when to stop, but that's the other side of the coin of a great sense of humor. I was far from perfect myself. Being in love with someone doesn't mean you have to share every single opinion.

LAURA JEAN

I HAD AN HOUR BETWEEN SCHOOL AND MY FOOD-
town shift, so I headed over to the bleachers to
catch some rays. I wanted a gorgeous tan for the
Fling, and I was going to start early and take it
slow so, for once, I wouldn't peel. Maybe I'd go
to the beach this weekend, before the real hot
weather started.

The bleachers were in bright sunlight and I
squinted. There was some kind of track meet
going on—red and white Shorehaven colors and
some other team in yellow. There was a small
scattering of people on the benches; track never
draws a crowd. I was climbing up to the top when
I saw Mrs. Delaney in the third row.

"Hi, Mrs. D!"

"Well, hello! What are you up to?"

"Just killing time. I don't go to work until
four." I sat down next to her.

"Ginny's in the one hundred and the long
jump."

Mrs. Delaney and Scott's dad, too—when he wasn't working—came out for all their kids' events, even the minor ones that no one bothered about. They were really caring and involved, always rooting for their kids to be winners.

"Who's the other team?" I asked.

"Glen Cove."

A woman at the far end of our row was struggling to keep a toddler from climbing farther up. He sure was a handful.

"I can't stay for the long jump," Mrs. Delaney said. "I have to meet a client. It's Ginny's best event, and I don't know why they always make it last!"

Mrs. D worked in real estate and Scott said that even in the slowest market, she just kept right on making sales. I could see that she'd be great at it. She was a lot like Scott, with lots of energy and charm. Tommy was different. He was the quiet one in the family. I wasn't sure if he was shy or if he didn't like me that much.

The starting gun went off for the 50-yard dash. A black Glen Cove girl came in first. Track was boring unless you were rooting for someone in particular.

"Working so much doesn't leave you enough

time for school activities," Mrs. Delaney said sympathetically. "That's too bad."

"That's not why I left the swim team," I said quickly. "I got tired of tasting chlorine all the time." I didn't *have* to work. It's not like we were poor or anything; our house wasn't *that* much smaller than the Delaneys'. Things were a little tight, that's all, after Anne's wedding. "Anyway, I think I'll quit when Scott gets through with baseball practice. So we'll have more time together before . . ."

I looked across the field. I wished I was wearing sunglasses to cover my eyes.

"I know." Mrs. Delaney took my hand. "We'll all miss him."

The girls were lining up for the second heat.

"He'll be coming home often." I tried for a bright smile. "Long weekends and—and holidays." I wanted to be bright and cheerful, like Mrs. D. I admired her a lot.

"That's not such a good idea." I saw a hint of a frown. "He'll have to concentrate on what he's doing and make use of this opportunity . . . Don't do anything to hold him back, Laura Jean."

"Hold him back?" I couldn't believe she was

saying that. Saying that with my hand still in hers.

"You're both moving on, to new contacts and—you know, there are lots of exciting new things ahead for you, too." She smiled that Scott-like smile, a little crooked, eyes sparkling. "Well, you know me, always being a mom! I only have his best interests at heart."

"So do I." I drew my hand away.

"I know you do, Laura Jean. So, woman-to-woman, don't make leaving too hard for him." Her lipstick was bright red and very shiny.

I was so surprised and hurt. I'd thought she was for us. She *liked* me, she'd told Scott I was a very nice girl, and Catholic, too . . . Maybe I was being paranoid and taking it the wrong way. We'd always had a great relationship; she'd even called me her other daughter. I rubbed my fingertips across the engraving on the heart bracelet. Scott loved me.

Mrs. Delaney stretched and looked around the stands. "Who is that? I know her from somewhere."

She was looking at a woman seated in front of us. Thin, pale, with wisps of blond hair escaping a rubber band.

Mrs. D leaned over. "Ellen Snowden?"

"Yes?"

"I *thought* it was you, I wasn't sure. Nora Delaney. It's been years, hasn't it?"

The woman looked puzzled.

"Tommy was in your daughter's class. Second grade, elementary school. I was class mother."

"Oh, yes, of course. How are you?"

"Just fine. That's my Ginny getting ready for the one hundred. The cute little redhead."

Mrs. Snowden glanced over and nodded appreciatively.

"Now where's Cathy?" Mrs. D asked.

"Cara. The blond ponytail on the side. Standing next to Mrs. Jensen." She paused and then, half shy, half proud, "She just won the second heat in the fifty."

"Good for her! You know, I always thought she was *such* a pretty little girl." Mrs. D always said nice things to people.

"Thank you." Mrs. Snowden was attractive when she smiled. She had good features, but she could have used some makeup. If I were doing her makeover, I'd put on lots of blusher and get her hair out of that rubber band. And her expression was too anxious when she wasn't smiling. I'm forever doing mental make-overs on people, I guess because I've worked so hard on myself.

The before-and-afters are my favorite articles in *Mademoiselle*.

"How's Tommy?" the woman was saying.

"Oh, you know, busy with his teams and things."

Tommy wasn't *that* busy. Baseball was winding down, and all he did was shadow Scott. He wasn't that good an athlete, either; he was just there.

"Cara's been spending all her time at track. With practices almost every afternoon."

"Oh, I know, the kids get so busy. Tommy just got his SAT scores—at least that pressure's off. He did well, so we're wondering if he even needs to take it again in the fall. Well, I guess Cara's going through the same thing?"

I could tell Mrs. D was itching to know Cara's score, to compare.

"No, Cara didn't take the SAT."

"Oh? I thought all the juniors—"

"She's a freshman," the woman said evenly.

Two years behind Tommy? I looked curiously at the woman. Had her kid been out sick for a long time or what? Something had to be wrong with her. She caught me staring.

"Oh, I thought—I didn't realize . . ." I could see Mrs. Delaney figuring it out, embarrassed, then a quick recovery. "Oh, then she must be with Ginny now . . . ," she said brightly.

"I suppose so."

An awkward silence.

Mrs. D found a quick change of subject. "Oh, I remember—you were a writer, weren't you?"

The woman nodded.

"It's so wonderful to be creative! Are you still writing?"

"Yes."

"Well, that's wonderful! Children's books, isn't it?"

"Yes." She turned back toward the field, her shoulders hunched over, folded in upon herself.

Mrs. Delaney looked at me, raised her eyebrows, and shrugged. I thought it was rude that the woman hadn't even appreciated Mrs. D being so friendly and covering up the awkwardness. I smiled back at Mrs. D. I wanted to feel close to her again. I really did.

CARA

"DID YOU SEE, MOMMY? DID YOU SEE? I WON THE second heat! I had the best time after that black girl. Mrs. Jensen said so. Mrs. Jensen said, next time—"

I like it that Mommy came. I can tell she's happy when I do good.

"They're going to say my name over the P.A. in school tomorrow. Mommy, Mrs. Jensen . . . By next year . . ."

I like walking home with her, but I'll bet anything the boys are still at the ball field. I'd like to hang out and watch them. But if I tell Mommy I don't want to go home yet, she'll say, "No, Cara, it's getting late," and I have to start on my homework before dinner. The meets take a long time. When it's just practice, I start running right after school and get all my laps done and the boys are still at the ball field and I can hang out with them and still get home before dinner.

I'm friends with the jocks. When someone says something snotty to me, I just think, *I'm special friends with Bob Dietrich and they're not,* and it doesn't hurt my feelings. Sometimes he and Scott Delaney and those guys ignore me, but sometimes they say "hi" to me. Monday I got to sit with them at lunch and we kidded around. The only one I don't like that much is John Masci because he's mean. My name is Snowden and Monday Bob was kidding around and calling me Slush-den. He said, "She's pure as the driven slush." He was paying attention to me and making jokes and stuff, but now Masci keeps calling me Slut-den and I don't like that.

When I was in second grade, I used to play with Emily and she lived right next door to Bob Dietrich. She moved away, but we used to ride our bikes in front of her house after school. Bob Dietrich would talk to us sometimes—he was in third grade then. He was nice to me. He let me pet his dog, Wolfie. He was my friend. Bob lives two blocks away from us, the big red brick house that I pass on the way to school. I've known him a long, long time. Scott and Tommy Delaney and Dan Gregory, too. They were on my elementary school bus. Bob never talked to me, except for those times when I was in second grade, but I got to be real friends with him last week. I even remember the exact day. It was the day after he got the end-of-year MVP. That means Most Valuable Player. There was a big awards dinner that was in all the papers, not only the Shorehaven paper.

Anybody would tell you that Bob Dietrich is very good-looking. His name was in all the papers, *Long Island Press* and all those, like he's a rock star. He's my favorite of all the jocks, and they're the coolest guys in school.

Anyway, it was the day after the awards dinner. The guys were still celebrating. They'd cut the afternoon. Valerie said they'd been drinking in the woods behind the school. Valerie said those jocks get away with everything—she bet they wouldn't even get cut slips. I was walking home after track practice with Anne. We were going across the parking lot. Sharon Miller was there, and Dina and Jennifer and Valerie. They were all talking to each other and forgetting about me. We saw the guys, so we stopped and watched them. Bob Dietrich looked pretty drunk. We were kind of leaning up against a parked car and watching. They came over. They were talking and stuff and the girls were flirting. Bob Dietrich kept going over to Sharon, almost on top of her, pinning her against the car. The other guys kept pulling him back, and she was laughing at him. He was saying stuff like "Hey, beautiful" and "C'mon, help me celebrate," and then he jumped at her and stuck his hands on her tits and yelled "Touchdown!" She stood up straight, real fast, and slapped his arms away and said, "Get him away from me!" The guys pulled him away, and he just stood there with his arms at his sides and he was saying, "What's so terrible? I want to touch your tits, that's all," and Scott Delaney was saying, "Hey, man, chill out," and laughing at him. Jennifer said, "Drunk as a skunk." Bob Dietrich looked very sad. He said, "What's the big deal? It's no big deal." He looked around at all of us, real sad, and said, "Who's going to let me feel their boobs? For one freakin' second?" So I said, "I will," because everyone was laughing at him, and I wanted to be friends with him.

He said for a second, but he held one in each hand and rubbed my nipples with his thumbs and all of a sudden, I got that prickly feeling right at the bottom of my tummy, like I sometimes do in class when I should be paying attention but I get that feeling and can't think about anything else.

I heard Anne say, "Cara! Let's go!" but I couldn't move, with that feeling and his hands on me, and then Anne said, "Come on, leave her alone. You know she's retarded," and that made me feel bad, but his hands were making me feel so good, and then Anne said, "That's so gross! Cara, come on. Are you coming?"

I was mad at her for spoiling everything and saying that before and I said, "No! Mind your own business! Don't stick your big fat bitch nose in my business!"

Scott Delaney yelled, "Way to go, Cara!" like he was on my side. He's nice.

So the girls went away and Bob kind of moved me around so he could get behind me and lean on the parked car. He had his arms around me from the back with his hands on my tits and then I could feel his thing all hard rubbing against my backside and I felt funny because all the guys were watching me. I could feel Bob breathing hard against my neck and I could smell the beer on his breath and then he said, "Let's go in the woods," so I said, "OK."

We left the guys in the parking lot and we walked to the woods behind the school. He was staggering drunk. I helped him walk. His arm was around my shoulders. It was romantic. I couldn't believe I was with Bob Dietrich! We went in a ways and then off the path, and then we lay down and he was on top of me and I could feel little sticks and stuff digging in my back and he was real heavy, but I didn't care, he was kissing me with his tongue in my mouth and I was tasting the beer in his mouth. I don't like beer 'cause it's too bitter, but I didn't care 'cause he was doing all this stuff and my heart was thumping so hard. He pulled my shorts down to my knees and then he pulled my blue panties down, too, and I started to pull them up because it felt funny getting naked outside, but then he started rubbing me down there and it was something like when I touch myself in bed at night, only better and a whole lot different. Mommy said never to touch myself in public, but it's OK in private. I used to forget sometimes and do it in public, but I don't anymore. Bob doing that was something like the same, but it was all different, too, and then he unzipped his jeans and took his thing out and stuck it in me and pushed and pushed. It hurt and his belt buckle scraped against my tummy, but some of it felt nice and I was happy because I had a boyfriend to love like Anne and Valerie—and it was Bob Dietrich! A boyfriend isn't like the bakery man. Then he passed out and I couldn't wake him; I tried to wake him for a long time. He pushed me away and said, "Go 'way," so I didn't know what to do. I pulled my shorts up and I went home.

I almost wanted to tell Mommy when I got home because I was so happy, but it's my own private property. I like something private that Mommy doesn't know about. Mommy wants to know every single thing.

She asked why I was late. I said because I did extra laps and then stopped for a soda with the girls. My blue panties had blood spots. I put them in the hamper in the middle of the towels. If Mommy sees, I'll say I got my period. She might be mad, and anyway, I'm not supposed to go in the woods.

I say "hi" to Bob Dietrich in the hall at school. I got to sit at their table at lunch on Monday.

JOE LOPEZ

I never saw Bob Dietrich get that wasted.
He couldn't walk. That's John Masci and Charlie
Goren just about every Saturday night, but it
was funny to see "Mr. Perfect" getting human.
He thinks he's too good to get down and dirty
with the rest of us. We were celebrating in the
woods that afternoon, and everybody was saying
wait till Dietrich got to Boston, he'd show Bean-
town the kind of player we grow in Shorehaven.
Well, something had him uptight—he kept hitting the bottle like there was no tomorrow. Man,
he was *green* at lunch the next day. We kept
sticking this plate of wiggling purple Jell-O in
front of his face.

"Cut it out!" he said, and then, to Masci, "If
I puke, it's gonna be all over your shoes."

That was a rank on Masci. Last year, he made
it with this dead-drunk broad at Clay's party.
Me, I wouldn't go for that; I got too much pride

in myself and anyway, I never have any problem getting girls. Well, right after Masci did it, she puked all over his new Nikes. For weeks after, if we wanted to get Masci mad, all we had to do was make gagging noises.

This time Masci laughed. It don't get to him anymore because that was a long time ago and, anyway, he's seeing Tina now. She's a nice girl, the cutest that's ever gone for him. Masci's my best friend on the team. Underneath he's got a good heart and I'd stand up for him anytime, but the truth is, on the outside, he's a slob and a clown. The truth is, Tina's too cute for him, but she's only a sophomore and I guess anybody on varsity football is a big deal.

Clay was yelling, "Watch it, Masci, he's about to let go! Watch your shoes!"

Masci just laughed.

Then Scott said to Bob, "So how was she?"

Bob looked embarrassed as hell. "Who?"

"*Who?* Who do you think? Cara."

I saw the muscle in Bob's cheek twitch. "Nothing happened," he mumbled.

"Too drunk to get it up, huh?" Scott said.

"Oh, I got it up all right!"

I was watching Bob's face, wondering what the truth was. Scott kept needling him and wouldn't let Bob squirm away. It was funny as hell. What did he think, he was too good to get it from anyone but the Queen of England? Listen, I'm the first to say Dietrich is a great athlete, but all this stuff Coach and everybody keep saying about he's a natural leader . . . He's not *my* leader. Mama's friend Consuela had a job babysitting for Bob when he was *twelve*. Consuela said it was because his parents were always away, but so what? Hell, when I was twelve, I was taking care of my three little sisters while Mama worked. I was the man in the family. I'm tougher than him, and I know a lot more about real life.

Yeah, I could have been the leader, if my situation was different. Can't wait to get in that flyboy uniform. In that U.S. uniform, I'm gonna start out equal with everyone else, clean slate, making good money, and then we'll see who's a natural leader. I'm the toughest guy on the team, well, maybe except for Clay. But Mike Clay's garbage.

I almost killed him one night. We were having some beers in the Delaneys' den, and Clay was plastered and sounding off about the illegals living ten to a room down by the railroad station. He was laughing about the time he went into an apartment house hallway in the middle of the night, yelling, "*Mira! Mira!* Immigration!"

"You oughta seen those spics scatter like

roaches." He laughed. "It was a freakin' riot!"

I was gonna haul off and kill him, but Masci pulled me off him and got me out of there. "Come on, chill out, he's drunk. Anyway, he didn't mean you." Masci walked me around the block to calm me down. I said a lot of those illegals were politicals, they were *somebody* in their own country. I said that girl Eliana had seen her own uncle drawn and quartered, it took real guts for her to just live normal, and the whole bunch of them better keep their mouths off the Latina girls. Masci apologized; he never thought it bothered me, they forgot all about me being Hispanic; I was one of the guys.

"Clay *likes* you, he's your buddy, he's a dumb ox, he wasn't thinking. Anyway, you're nothing like those losers that hang around the station."

"Moron," I said. "*I* live in one of the buildings down there." But he said, "Come on, Joe, you're different, you know what I mean." I knew what he meant, I was a "Good Spic." But we talked for a long time that night, and Masci listened to me. John Masci is an OK guy. He told me a lot of stuff about himself, too. And it don't hurt to be good friends with the mayor's son.

One time, I'm hanging out in front of my building with some people when a police car drove up. Seems somebody had thrown a rock through the picture window at the library. It wasn't us, but they started hassling us. We're just standing there on our own block, and we're hassled by a bunch of Keystone Kops! I got mad and someone started shoving, and it was turning into a bad scene. But then Mayor Masci drove up; he saw me and he said, "That's Joe Lopez— he's all right." And they left us alone. "Take it easy, son," he said to me.

I hate Mike Clay, but the truth is he's there for me on the football field. I've got to say that for Clay—he's no showboat. He'll sacrifice and be right where you need him. He's a rock. Bob Dietrich's the one who always has to be a hot-shot.

But he wasn't feeling that hot now. Cara had come into the cafeteria. She was standing there, staring over at our table like some lost soul.

"Here comes your puppy now," Scott said.

"OK, Delaney," Bob said between clenched teeth. "That's enough. Joke's over."

Scott thought it was so funny, he couldn't let it go. "Hey, Cara, come here, sit next to Dietrich. He wants you next to him!"

She came trotting over, and we all made room for her next to Bob. I never saw such a dumb slut. She was bouncing around in her chair, hyper as hell, and laughing at anything anyone said. "Hey, Cara, you look like a fresh egg . . . Just laid." You could say *anything* to her and all she did was flip her hair and lean up against Bob like a cat in heat.

He must've done something right for her, because everyone noticed Cara hanging around the baseball field for the rest of that week. I even saw her following him in the hall. Man, she was begging for more!

No one invited her, but Cara started automatically plopping down at our table. Bob's trying to sic her on Goren and Delaney. Looks like we'll never get rid of her; you can't insult her, no matter what. This one time Annette was sitting with us, and when she heard what they were saying to Cara, she started lacing into Bob about letting the guys talk that way in front of *her*, and he said, "Don't tell me what to do!" and the next thing you know, she was screaming at him.

I guess Bob's doing it with her, but if you ask me, it's not worth it, even if she's a model or something. She's an icy bitch. This girl I'm seeing, Carmen, is built a million times better and she's a real woman, too. She knows how to treat a man. I was thinking of taking her to the Fling, but she might not fit in that good. Annette would look down her nose at Carmen. I don't know about Tina or L.J. L.J.'s nice, she's real— none of that phony, giggly shit about her . . . Hell, I'll take anyone I damn please!

I heard Bob telling Scott that Annette *ordered* him to get her white orchids for the Fling because that's the only thing that would go with her dress, and Bob told Scott he might have anyway, but he didn't like being pushed.

"Yeah," Scott said. "She's too beautiful. She thinks any guy's gonna jump through hoops when she snaps her fingers."

"I'm tired of performing for everybody," Bob said. "I'm tired. Sick and tired!" He sounded like he was losing it. I don't get it. This is a guy that's got everything handed to him, so what's his problem?

LAURA JEAN

IF YOU TELL SOMEONE SOMETHING THEY DON'T want to hear, even if it's for their own good, they are likely to turn on you. No one likes the messenger. But I was willing to take the chance because Pat's been my best friend ever since third grade, when I was new in school and she'd been assigned to show me around, and it hurt to see the way that jerk was treating her. Ron Gilbert was arrogant and he wasn't even a jock, but for some reason, he awed her. He got into Harvard, which is fine, but Pat had been so up about getting into the University of Vermont—it's not that easy for out-of-staters—and he did everything to spoil it for her. "The Ivies are a *real* education and the rest are only pseudocolleges." That was uncalled for and so typical of him.

I was walking down the hall with Pat and she was telling me about the latest outrageous way he'd put her down. She was almost in tears, so I pulled her into the girls' room.

"You don't need this," I said.

Pat blew her nose.

"Why don't you start hanging out with us again?" I kept my voice low because there were some other girls in the bathroom. "Come out with me and Scott tonight; I think Charlie Goren likes you and—"

Her eyes widened. "You don't understand. I'm not breaking up with him! It was just a little argument, it was nothing. I thought I could *talk* to you without . . ." She turned from me and smashed the tissue into the wastepaper basket; the swinging top rattled.

"We should talk," I said, "because—" I took a deep breath. There was a lot I had to say.

"Hi, Laura Jean!" A girl was next to me, looking into the mirror, her reflection smiling at me. I didn't know her from Adam. I acknowledged her with a nod.

"—because, Patty," I continued, "someone else can see things more objectively and—"

Pat turned on the sink water full force, drowning me out. I waited while she washed her face.

The girl at the mirror had taken down her ponytail and was brushing her long blond hair. She fluffed out the ends, admiring herself, like she thought she was Rapunzel.

"Laura Jean? You're so lucky you go out with Scott," she said to me. "He's nice. I like Scott next best after Bob. Don't you think they're both so handsome? I'm keeping my fingers crossed that Bob will—"

"Lots of luck," I muttered. Who was she anyway? Another one who wanted to make points with Bob through me? I interrupted her babbling. "Let's go," I said to Pat. It was so weird. I didn't even know her.

Out in the hall, I asked, "Who was that?"

"Cara something," Pat said. "John Masci and Bob Dietrich and those guys fool around with her at lunch."

"What do you mean, fool around?"

"Pass her from lap to lap, stupid things like that. She has this really obnoxious high-pitched voice, so everyone in the whole cafeteria hears her."

Scott would be at that table. "Scott, too?" It was rotten that I didn't have lunch with him this semester.

"Well, yeah, I guess he's there."

"How long has that been going on?"

"I don't know, a week maybe." Pat glanced at me. "Wait a minute, it's nothing—they're just playing with her. There must be something wrong with her—she has this giggle, and a screech, I swear, like fingernails on a blackboard!"

I had to stop getting those flutters of jealousy. Over nothing. Pat had picked up on it and glossed it over for me; she was my friend.

"I still think we should talk about—"

"No, I'm fine," she said. She hugged her books against her chest.

"You weren't so fine a minute ago."

"You don't know Ron. It's because he's so brilliant; he gets impatient with me, that's all. I'm nowhere near as smart as he is, and that's a fact." She looked at the notices on the bulletin board in the hall; she wouldn't meet my eyes. "I'm too sensitive, that's all."

"You're not too sensitive." This was *Patty*, who'd dreamed of being a wild, free horse.

"Let's just forget it, OK?"

I knew Ron Gilbert was the first boy Pat had ever seriously been with. And I wanted to tell her what Teresa had said. It applied directly to Pat.

The way it came about was that, ages ago, Mom sat me down for that awful little talk. I was embarrassed; I had been sleeping with Scott for months by then.

"Laura Jean," Mom had said, "you know we like Scott—"

"I know." I had overheard her talking to her friend on the phone, making a point that I was going out with *Scott Delaney*. I could tell she was proud of that; everyone knew who he was.

"We like him a lot. But when you see so much of one boy . . . well, there are temptations . . ."

I cringed. "Don't worry," I said.

"So be careful not to let things get out of control—it's up to the girl to keep things in control . . . to set limits . . ."

If it hadn't been so embarrassing, it would have been funny. I mean, really, she should have guessed by now. "We're not doing anything," I mumbled.

"Well, OK then," she said. She sounded relieved that she was almost finished. "Scott is a boy that's going places, he's a real catch, but you have to be smart—if he can get all the milk he wants for free, he's not going to buy the cow."

"The *cow?*" I exploded. "That's out of Victorian times!"

She gave me a sharp look. "You don't know it all, Laura Jean! Take it from me—that's the way men are."

It was ridiculous. She didn't know anything about the way it was between Scott and me. It was too ridiculous to even think about. Next thing, I'd hear about a stitch in time saves nine and don't put all your eggs in one basket. It had nothing to do with anything, but the next time Teresa was over, I couldn't help mentioning it.

Teresa's my oldest sister. I'm the youngest, with Anne and Mary in between. Teresa's married and has been out of the house for a long time, but somehow she's the one that I've always been closest to. I've always been able to talk to her.

"You won't believe what Mom said to me." I repeated the conversation.

She laughed. "That sounds just like her."

"It came right out of the blue. Where does she get those things? I mean, doing it would make people even closer, right?"

"Sometimes it does and sometimes it doesn't. Depending on what else is going on with them."

"That's what I thought."

Teresa studied me. "Are you having sex with Scott, Laura Jean?"

I hesitated. Then, "Yes."

She sighed. "You're so young."

"We're in love," I said quickly.

Teresa nodded. "I know."

"We were dating for almost two years before—
I mean, what does she expect? It's only natural
to— It's not *wrong*— Teresa?"

"You've got a tiger by the tail," she said. "Especially when it's the first boy you've ever been
with, you think he *invented* sex. It's hard to separate that from love . . ."

"I wouldn't want to," I said. "Why would I
want to?"

"What I'm trying to say is—sex can be so
powerful and blinding . . ."

I remembered that conversation and it applied
perfectly to Pat.

"Pat," I said, "Please. Listen to what I have
to say. Because that's what friends are for."

She stopped walking and leaned against the
hall wall. She looked tired. "I know what you're
going to say. You don't like Ron. But I love
him."

"That's just the point. How do you *know* you
love him? It's your first experience, and you've
got that all mixed up with love. Maybe you're
talking yourself into love, just to justify—"

I didn't expect Pat to get so angry. "How do
you know you love Scott?" she snapped. "He's
your first, so what do you know? Thanks a whole

lot for all the wisdom. I'm going to English!"
She stalked off.

That's what I got for trying to help. I was
offended that she'd even tried to put me in that
same high school crush category. I *knew*. Scott
was the great love of my life!

CARA

I'M ON MY WAY TO THE STAIRCASE FOR HOME economics. I see Bob Dietrich standing with that girl Annette at the hall lockers. She's yelling at him. I don't like her. She was snotty to me at lunch that time and mean to Bob, too. I don't like yelling. When someone yells at me, it makes me cry.

All of a sudden, Bob slams his locker door hard. I can hear it echo down the hall. He's lucky he didn't get his hand caught. That happened to me once. It hurt so bad and my nail turned black. He walks away from her and he looks mad. He doesn't like her, either. He's walking real fast, so I go in front of him where he can see me and I say, "Hi, Bob."

He goes right by me, so I follow him and I say, "Hi, Bob."

That girl made him mad.

I have to hurry to keep up with him. "Where're you going?"

"Nowhere," he says.

"You have to be going *somewhere*," I say.

I have to rush to keep up with him. He walks so fast.

"Can I go with you? Can I?"

I don't like home economics. I like the apple sauce and I know how to make it so it tastes good with lots of cinammon. I don't like the measuring, with quarter ounces and half pints.

"OK," he says. He's talking between his teeth. "You want to give me a blow job?"

I know what that means. I hear the girls talk.

"OK." I wish he would smile at me. He has nice teeth.

He grabs my arm. I have to skip to keep up with him. He pulls me down the stairs to the gym.

I don't know why they call it a blow job, because you don't blow anything, like blowing up a balloon or blowing on hot soup.

We go in the storage room. I've never been in here. It smells like leather and ointment. He pulls me into the corner behind the shelves. It's dark back here. I'm excited to be all alone with Bob Dietrich in the dark.

I think he's going to kiss me and touch me like the other time, but he pushes me down to my knees. "Hurry up. Come on, come on, hurry up, somebody could come in here." I hear his zipper.

It's not like the bakery man. Bob is my boyfriend.

I like the way he's breathing and getting all excited and everything, and it's making me feel like that. The part I don't like is when he shoves it so far back in my mouth. I almost gag and I don't want him to get mad.

After, he doesn't talk or walk me to class or anything. He's moody. Mommy says my cousin Sue is moody.

I know Bob likes the way I did it for him, because two other times he takes me down there in a big rush because he wants me to do it again.

When I sit with Bob and Scott and those guys at lunch, they pay attention to me. It's so much fun. Sometimes I forget to eat. They say funny things to me and we laugh. Not Bob, so much, because he doesn't talk to me much. Scott is very good-looking, too. He fools around with me a lot. One time, Scott pulled me on his lap. I stayed there for a long time and I could feel his thing get hard because of me. If I move around on someone's lap, their thing gets hard. Then the lunchroom teacher yelled at me to get off and sit on a chair. I made a face at her and everyone laughed. I like Scott a whole lot. He used to say "dummy" to me on the bus, but he's nice now. I like Charlie Goren, too. I was sitting next to Charlie and he put my hand on his thing under the table and whispered in my ear. We went under those stairs that go up to the balcony of the auditorium and then I was late to math, but not that late.

After track practice, I go over to the ball field and watch the guys. I look at the way they move. I hope they'll hang out with me when they get through. But then Bob said, "Come on, let's get going," and they all left.

Yesterday I was wearing my yellow shirt and a yellow ribbon in my hair. I told Mommy I always want a ribbon to match. I have pretty hair, too, because it's long and blond, and now I wear it loose so everyone can see.

LAURA JEAN

I WAS IN THE SIN BIN. THAT'S ROOM 103, WHERE you have to put in a certain number of hours as punishment. I had to give up four free periods—today was one, tomorrow I had two, Friday one more, and then I'd finally be finished with this. It was a beautiful day and I knew everybody was outside under the big oak. I was longing for the smell of grass and the sunshine on my skin, actually *craving* it.

The deal was, if I turned in a five-page written report on the digestive system of invertebrates and did four periods, Mr. Held wouldn't fail me for the last quarter. But I was sitting slouched way back, sulking, resentful as anything because I still thought I was right. I knew I was.

Mrs. Rosen had sin duty this period. She was at the desk in front of the room, reading. She looked just about as bored as I was. I could have been doing homework, but I didn't feel like it. I wanted out!

Tommy Delaney only got one period for punching Alex Maitland in the face. It happened in the cafeteria and the lunchroom teacher saw it. I don't think walking out of Held's class was any worse than that. Maybe a fight is in the boys-will-be-boys category and what I did was subversive. Who knows?

I looked around the room. Almost everybody was staring off into space. Nobody I wanted to sit with or talk to. This was a complete waste and I didn't know what it was supposed to prove.

Tommy Delaney was pretty quiet and usually didn't get into trouble. It started with something about cutting the hot food line, but Tommy was definitely picking a fight. Alex Maitland was the only *real* gay that I knew about; he was so swishy, you just couldn't miss it. There were kids around school that everybody called fags, but actually they were just wimps. Like the chorus fags. Charlie Goren has a great voice, but he wouldn't be caught dead in chorus. Tommy hates gays in the worst way; I don't know why he feels *that* strong about it. One of these days, he's going to pulverize Alex. Alex's eye was swelling and he was feeling around his nose, to see if it was broken. I felt kind of sorry for him, but he didn't even try to fight back.

I shifted my weight and my seat creaked.

The door opened and Dan Gregory came in. He checked in with Mrs. Rosen and she said something about his being late, so maybe it shouldn't count toward his time, and he said, "Come on, I had to come all the way from the other side of the building . . ." She yawned and said, "All right."

Dan scoped the room for someone he knew; he sat down next to me.

"At least I shaved five minutes off," he said. "What're you in for?"

"Oh, it's too stupid and complicated to go into." I sighed. "What did you do?"

"I keep missing homeroom. I don't know, I just can't get there. One period sin bin."

"I got four."

"Oh, wow," he said. "You must've *sinned!*"

"Yeah, really."

Mrs. Rosen glanced over at us. "Keep it down."

"So," Dan whispered, "what did you do? Throw a Molotov cocktail at the guidance office?"

"Not quite."

"Yeah, but you're doing serious time, Laura Jean. I know! You put itching powder in The Munchkin's crotch!"

That made me smile.

"*Ummmm* . . . Acid in the water coolers?"

"You're psychotic," I said, laughing.

"True, but I'm not the one in heavy-duty incarceration. Who'd have thought. A nice girl like you."

"I got in trouble with Mr. Held and his snake circus."

"Oh, him. Sadistic bastard."

Mrs. Rosen raised her eyebrows at us. "Keep it down," she said in a monotone.

I ran my finger along the letters carved into the wooden desktop. "2 Live Crew." "Madonna."

Dan yawned.

I checked the wall clock. Forty minutes to go. I studied the peeling paint on the ceiling.

Dan yawned and stretched. "Hey, did Scott ever tell you about his Hiroshima report?"

"Hiroshima? I forgot all about that. What did he do?"

"Man, I should've put it on tape! The problem is, when something funny happens, it's all over before I can even get the camcorder out."

"What did he do?"

"OK. Long shot: a bunch of social studies

classes crammed into the all-purpose room, the teachers and the head of the department sitting at a long table. This is the big project for the term, mega-serious atmosphere. One kid after another in front of the room, droning through six-, seven-page reports. Sound track: monotone voices, repetitions, coughs. Close-up: one of the teachers stifling a yawn."

Dan was OK, he was funny, but his movie-talk sounded too put-on to me.

"Then it's Scott's turn. I'm sitting there wondering what he'll do. Well, he went into the library just before class and photocopied a picture of Hiroshima after the bomb. It was grim, pure devastation. So he marches up to the front of the room with this picture in his hand. He holds it up. He goes to the kids in the front row and shows it to them, one by one. Then he goes over to the teachers and sticks it in each of their faces for long, weighted moments. Another pregnant pause and he stretches his arms out, total drama, and says, 'Need I say more?' And then he sits down!"

"That's it, he sits down!" Dan started chortling. "The end, *finis*. There was this stunned silence and then everyone breaks up and even the chairman of the department cracks a smile.

Your boyfriend's got great style, L.J. Who else could pull that off?"

I shook my head and smiled. That was Scott, all right; he had style. "Is he going to pass, do you think?"

"Oh sure," Dan said. "Listen, they have to give him *something* for originality."

Mrs. Rosen was staring at us. "You two, stop talking. This isn't a social hour."

Dan shrugged and pulled out a book.

I wished I'd been there to see him. But sometimes I almost thought they let Scott get away with too much for his own good. Scott was smart—he could memorize anything a million times faster than me—but no one made him buckle down. I guess that was all right, because he needed his time for sports, and hockey got him into Dartmouth, didn't it?

But sometimes it seemed that I was learning about things and there were big gaps in what he knew. Like when I was upset about the Holocaust, and I wanted to talk to him about it.

"Holocaust?" He frowned. "Isn't that some kind of Jewish holiday?"

I was taking a class called Holocaust studies. To tell the truth, I was in that class by accident. I knew what the Holocaust was, and I wasn't especially interested in it. But I needed a social studies elective and the only other one that fit into my program was at nine o'clock in the morning. So I took Holocaust.

We saw those terrible photographs: children's shoes piled up into a huge pyramid, mounds of bodies thrown every which way on top of each other . . . It seemed unreal. Big numbers like six million numb me. But then a woman came to talk to us and suddenly the numbers had names and ages. She lives in Shorehaven, and you'd never know she was a survivor of anything. She looked like anybody else in town, grayish-blond hair in a French knot. She only had a slight accent. She works for the dentist on lower Main Street.

She told us about when she was twelve years old and separated from her family, crammed against the side of a boxcar bumping along the rails. She couldn't think about anything but her thirst. Thirst is worse than starvation, she said. There was a space between the planks, big enough to see out and to get her hand through. The train stopped for a moment near a small German town and she could see snow on the embankment. All she could think of was water. A middle-aged townswoman was walking along the side with a small dog, almost close enough to touch. She stretched her hand out through the slats and begged, "Please. Snow." The woman's answer was, "Damn the Jew-bitch who bore you." She was still childlike and trusting enough then, she said, to feel shocked.

Then the teacher took over and said ordinary people can complacently do evil when they dehumanize "the other." In My Lai, he said, nice, regular American guys could massacre babies because the Vietnamese were "gooks," not quite human. It was important for us to understand, he said, so that it won't keep happening over and over again. Two of the girls in the class cried.

I needed to talk to somebody about it. "So it's sad," Scott said, "but why keep bringing up ancient history?" I guess I'm not as eloquent as the teacher.

All the talk about "the other" made me uncomfortable and I don't know why. I've never done anything deliberately cruel in my whole life. I'm not like that, and neither are any of the people I know.

LAURA JEAN

WELL, I GOT DAD TO GIVE ME MONEY FOR THE Fling dress. Sometimes when Mom's annoyed with me, she says I'm a master manipulator; I don't think that's true. Anyway, I've heard Mom say herself that you have to know how to get around a man.

"Daddy," I said, "I'll understand if it's a problem, but . . . All those Ocean Point girls are going to be all dolled up and everyone's getting something new and . . . You know, most of the girls have their own credit cards, in their own names . . . It's just, everyone can tell a *bridesmaid's* dress, like we can't even afford to . . ."

I saw Dad wavering.

"It's OK if you can't," I said. "Don't worry about it. I know Scott likes me for myself; he'll understand if I can't be well dressed . . ."

There was no way Dad could take that, so he wound up giving me a roll of bills. I wasn't feeling very proud of myself, but—hey, combined with my Foodtown savings, I could get something truly spectacular! And it was Saturday morning, so I had time to shop till I dropped.

"God, I'm carrying more cash than I've ever had at one time in my life," I said to Pat. She was driving us to Miracle Mile, with just one detour; I had to pick up last week's pay from Foodtown on the way.

Pat pulled up at the delivery ramp.

"I'll be out in a flash."

Ted, the manager, had my envelope ready.

"Can you take Janice's shift on Monday? She has some kind of conflict."

"Yeah, OK," I said.

"So I'll switch you to Monday afternoon and give her Tuesday?"

"OK, no problem."

"Good. Thanks." Then he started chatting about something or other. He can be so long-winded.

"Someone's waiting for me . . . gotta run," I said. "See you Monday."

"Rush, rush, rush," he called after me. "Always rushing."

I squeezed past the long lines at the check-out. Saturdays were always the most crowded.

"Hi, Laura Jean!"

It was that blond girl.

"Mommy, that's Laura Jean Kettering."

The woman from the track meet—Mrs. Snowden. She was wheeling a full food cart. So this was her daughter.

"Oh. Hi."

"What're you doing today, Laura Jean? Want to hang out? Where's Scott?"

"Uh—I don't know." I kept moving past her.

"She could come over for lunch, right, Mommy?"

"Sorry, I've got to go," I mumbled.

Pat still had the motor running, and I hopped into the car. "Let's rock 'n' *roll!*"

Pat made a right turn out of the parking lot. "Where first?"

"Lord & Taylor's. They have the best stuff."

"If we don't find anything at L&T, let's try A&S," Pat said.

"And have lunch at I-HOP. L&T, A&S, I-HOP—that's the code for the day."

Pat laughed. We were whizzing along the Boulevard.

"Remember the girl from the bathroom that day? Something Snowden?"

"Cara. Cara Snowden."

"She thinks she *knows* me. She wants to hang out. I don't know why she keeps talking to me."

"What?"

"I just saw her in the store."

"She's a mega-slut."

"Oh, come on . . ."

"No, really." Patty lowered her voice. "Someone saw Bob hustling her down to the supply room."

"Bob Dietrich? No way."

"I swear to God. She's fooling around with everybody. Going down on the whole school. Charlie Goren, too."

"How do you know?"

"I heard it from Margo. The word gets around."

"Oh, everyone's always starting rumors. If that was true about Dietrich, Scott would have said something."

"You think he tells you everything?"

"He does," I said.

Pat took her attention from the road for a second and gave me a look, eyebrows raised.

I wanted to tell her she didn't understand how close and honest a relationship could be, but since that flare-up about Ron Gilbert, I had to be careful.

"She might be retarded," I said. "I mean, that's pathetic. Dietrich wouldn't—"

"She doesn't look retarded," Pat said. "They have those funny eyes."

"She used to be in Tommy Delaney's class and now she's two years behind him."

"So, she's dumb."

"What if she's really retarded, though?" I said.

"She's not. She goes to a regular high school, doesn't she?"

"I guess . . ."

"If there's nothing at Miracle Mile, let's try Bloomie's," Pat said. "I want to feel like I'm in a rose garden. Pink and red roses on silk, yards and yards of skirt, and a red velvet ribbon. There was a picture in *Elle* . . ."

"I want slinky—strapless and straight slinky black, well, maybe shoestring rhinestone straps and . . ."

Sometimes you don't really know what you want until it's right there in front of you, calling your name. First, we checked out the prom dresses in the junior department. They were insipid—pastel Little Bo-Peeps. The stupid bridesmaid's dress would have fit right in. So then we went to designer dresses, and there it was.

It was emerald green silk crepe, not black, and it wasn't strapless, but it was almost jumping off its hanger, calling "Laura Jean! Laura Jean!" It had a deep V neckline outlined with ruffles. It was long and straight, with the skirt coming up in front in an inverted V.

I tried it on. The skirt was clinging, it fit like a second skin, and then, in front, it came up to way above my knees with a whoosh of ruffles. It was like long and very short at the same time. I have good legs, they're my best feature. I took off my socks and sneakers and posed on my toes, to give the effect of high heels. Fantastic!

"What do you think?"

"It's great," Pat said. "That's a great color for red hair."

There's always that second of surprise when someone says I'm a redhead because I just started coloring my hair recently. It's not *red* red, more like auburn—but Pat was right, emerald green was my color.

"How about the neckline? Does it show too much?"

"No," Pat said. "There's nothing wrong with some cleavage."

I laughed. "If you've got it, flaunt it!"

I didn't have that much in the way of

cleavage, but I mostly liked my body; losing that extra weight had helped a lot. I didn't like my nose. I wished I had a perfect nose.

I turned this way and that in the mirror. I looked honest-to-God glamorous, I really did. I smiled at myself in the mirror. I held my hair up. God, it was a dream.

Pat looked at the price tag. "*Whoa*," she said.

"I love it," I said. "I'm getting it."

"But L.J.—for just one night?"

"When Scott's at Dartmouth, I bet they have formals there so I'll get more use out of it. And anyway, I *love* it."

Then even the salesgirl said, "Not too many people could wear that dress. It's made for you."

I had to have it, and the only way to buy something at that price was to plunge ahead and do it. I toted the package as I followed Pat around. She tried on at least a million things.

I'd have to get shoes dyed to match. Teresa had drop earrings with green stones; they'd be perfect, and I knew she'd lend them to me.

"This one's pretty." I helped Pat with the zipper. "It's nice on."

"My hips look big," Pat said.

"You don't even have big hips, Patty."

"Well, it makes me feel fat."

I could see Pat getting miserable about herself; she was hating the way she looked in everything.

"Let's just quit and have lunch," she finally said. "I don't feel like trying anything else."

"I'll go with you . . ."

"No, no, I can go to Bloomie's next week. There's still time."

Funny what a dress can do. Pat was way down, and happiness kept bubbling up in me—I couldn't help it. Last year, on the afternoon before the Fling, traffic had been jammed all along Main Street. There were long lines at all the florists, the beauty salons were filled, and you couldn't get into that nail place for anything. The whole town came to a standstill; you could feel the anticipation in the air. This year was my turn, and I had the perfect dress! I'd get silk wraps for my nails and a French manicure, and the guys would rent limos and get flowers. I'd get a red rosebud for Scott's boutonniere, that was classier than a carnation.

There's always that scramble, people getting together just to have a date for the Fling, with lots of last-minute compromises. It had to feel stupid to get all dressed up for someone you didn't even care about. I was so lucky. I was daydreaming about all my accessories and how I'd wear my hair and . . . I was just so happy!

When I look back on that Saturday now, all I can think about is Ted asking me to switch shifts. That's when my luck ran out. If I'd said no, if I hadn't worked that Monday afternoon . . . When baseball practice got canceled, Scott and I might have gone over to the Delaneys' and watched TV. If I hadn't been working, maybe none of it would have happened.

JOE LOPEZ

I WAS GLAD BASEBALL PRACTICE WAS CANCELED on Monday. It was hot and muggy, more like a July dog-day than May. Anyway, baseball's not my game; I'm in it mostly to hang with my friends.

The coach said he had some personal business to take care of, but since we had the field anyway, we should go over and use it. Charlie Goren pulled a hamstring the day before; he said it hurt and he drove home. A bunch of us went: me, the Delaneys, Bob Dietrich, John Masci, Mike Clay, Bluestein, Tim Hughes, and some of the younger boys—Donaldson, Greeley . . . We threw the ball from base to base in slow, lazy arcs. There was only one game left to the season, so no one cared that much.

I was sweating at second base. I jogged to the side behind home plate and pulled off my shirt.

"Joe!" Masci called.

"I'm out," I yelled back. I lay back next to the mesh fence and dropped my mitt on the grass.

"Come on, you lazy S.O.B.!"

"It's too damn hot," I called.

Scott flopped down next to me. We watched the guys going through the motions. At the far end of left field, there was a door cut in the mesh; someone was standing there. I squinted. That girl Cara.

"What's she waiting for?"

"You ever heard the saying, a woman's either a goddess or a doormat?" Scott suddenly slapped at his arm. "Got 'im!"

"Too early for mosquitoes," I said.

"Yeah? Tell it to this sucker." He pushed his sweatband back off his forehead. "Well, she's a doormat."

After a while, Masci, Clay, Tommy, and Bluestein came over.

"Too hot," Masci said.

"What was your first clue?" I said.

Bob Dietrich was talking to Tim at the pitcher's mound. "Hey, you guys!" he called over. "How about batting practice?" Mr. Natural Leader.

"Give it up, Dietrich," Scott said.

Cara waved at us. No one bothered to answer.

She stood at the door, waiting. She kept shifting from one foot to the other. From this distance, it looked like she was hopping.

Dietrich and the others came over. "Come on, we've still got Roslyn on Friday."

"Roslyn," Clay snorted. "We'll bury them with one arm tied behind us."

"So, what do you want to do?" Bob pulled off his T-shirt and wiped his face with it.

"What do *you* want to do?"

"I don't know."

"Nothing happening around here."

"This town is beat," Scott said.

I was thirsty. We'd probably wind up at the Delaneys' as usual, and I sure hoped they had some ice cold Cokes. And lots of ice cubes.

"So what are we doing?" Bluestein asked.

The sky was overcast and the air, thick with humidity, wasn't moving.

Scott stood up. "Yo, Cara!"

She looked at us. Scott beckoned her over.

"Oh, shit!" Bob said.

"Come on, we'll have some fun," Scott said.

She was walking across the diamond toward us. She walked slowly, hips swaying.

"We have to bring this stuff down to the storeroom," Bob said.

"You want to take Cara with you?" Scott said. We were all watching her walk. "You know you want to."

"Cut it out!" Bob was mad.

"What's the matter with you? What's the big secret? You think you're the only one she's sucked off?" Scott laughed. "Who else? Come on, just between us, who else?"

Bluestein grinned. "I heard Charlie—"

"Yeah, I know about him, who else?"

Masci cleared his throat. "One time."

"*You?* No kidding."

The younger boys were listening, bug-eyed. We watched her walk across the diamond.

"How come no one told me?" Mike Clay said.

And then Cara was standing there next to us. "Hi."

"Hi, Cara. How's tricks?" Mike Clay started laughing like a maniac. For a big guy, he has a weird high-pitched laugh.

"What're you guys doing?" she asked. "Are you through with practice? What are you doing now?"

Mike Clay stood close to her. "Maybe we'll have a party." He snatched at the ends of her hair. "You want to party?"

"OK," Cara said.

"Say it," Scott said. "Say 'I want a get-laid party.'"

Cara hesitated and looked up at Scott. Clay was pawing her.

Scott kneaded the back of her neck. "You're with friends. It'll be funny."

"I want a get-laid party." She giggled.

"Say 'I'm horny,'" Masci told her.

"I'm horny." She giggled again.

And then the other guys were yelling out things for her to say, the crudest words they knew, and she parroted everything, giggling, things they could do to her, looking at the faces crowded around her, things she would do to them, giggling and looking pleased at the laughs. It was kind of funny in a dumb way. You know what it was like? It was like my kid sister Mercedes, when she was real little, shouting "Doo-doo!" and "Big doody!" And if anyone laughed, she'd never stop. But Cara was no toddler. She was hopping around, and I stared at her bouncing boobs.

I was getting turned on in spite of myself. "This is stupid."

"Yeah." Bob's voice was thick. "Let's get the stuff put away and go over to Scott's."

"Me, too?" she asked.

"Can I come to your house?" she said. "I'm coming, right?"

"Yeah, OK," Scott said.

"No, you're crazy," Tommy stage-whispered. "What about Mom and Ginny?"

"They're at the dentist. They're not getting home before dinner."

We had the whole afternoon stretching ahead.

Tim Hughes and those guys had tagged along; there were ten of us crowded in the Delaneys' family room. We were jammed together, standing in a tight almost-circle, inhaling each other's sweat and breath. Cara, stark naked, was in the middle. Not a stitch on. Once the music stopped, she stood still. She had her shoulders hunched forward and her arms folded in front of her chest.

Something was about to go down. I knew it. And I was thinking, *How did it get this far?*

When we first got to the Delaneys', Scott put some tapes on, some rap. Cara was dancing in front of us. She's not a good dancer. She was throwing herself around, rotating her hips, her face flushed. It was stupid and boring.

"Let's do something," I said.

Everyone was getting restless; the big joke was

over. The girl is an asshole. She went on dancing, looking for attention; she didn't know when to quit. Then somebody said, "Take it off!" She kept on hopping around to the beat. Scott said, "Hey Cara, do a strip. Show us what you got," and she looked at him. "It's OK, we're all friends here," he said. And then everybody was chanting "Take it off! Take it off!" and clapping. I could see her getting excited being in the center of it, everyone watching and laughing and egging her on. I could tell she was getting a kick out of the reaction every time something got unbuttoned.

"Jeeze," Tim Hughes breathed, "she does anything you tell her."

"Maybe we better not . . . ," one of the younger guys said.

If it ever comes to that, I can swear on a stack of Bibles that she took every stitch off by herself. Scott may have been screwing with her mind, but she took everything off by herself.

She was hyper as anything, giggling and showing off. Her face was flushed and shiny.

When she got to pulling down her underpants, the kidding around stopped. She was awkward, pulling them over her socks and sneakers, and trying to keep the beat. She's a natural blond. I never saw anybody that light. I was riveted.

Then the tape ran down. She stood there in

the sudden silence. It was strange, all of us dressed normal except her. She hunched her shoulders and shivered. Her patch was silky, no kinks. The rain had started—rain pelting the window glass, water gurgling from the drainpipe outside. The whir from the tape deck.

"Who goes first?" Clay said.

Her head made quick, birdlike movements. Her eyes darted from Scott to Bob and back to Scott. Dietrich was squeezed in next to me. He nudged me with a hoarse, nervous laugh. "Go for it, José. Here's your shot at an American."

That cut me loose. I turned stone cold. Whatever had been bonding me to these guys fell away like a fever breaking. I was Joe Lopez. I was joining the Air Force. It flashed through my mind that once school was over, I'd never see any of them again and I didn't much care. I didn't need this Screw-a-Retard Brotherhood.

I was drenched by the time I got to the apartment. Mercedes was home, writing in her loose-leaf at the kitchen table. She looked up at me with a quick smile. "Hi."

"Hi, yourself."

"You're soaked. You're gonna get sick."

"Naw, not me."

She bent back over her book. She's smart as a whip, always doing her homework. Smart and beautiful, too. She looks like that movie star Demi Moore. She'll be OK.

I used to take care of her when Mama had that second job on weekends. I was left in charge. My other two sisters were nine and ten, so they didn't need me that much. Mercedes was only five and I had to do everything for her. She was pretty good; she looked up to me and paid attention to what I told her. But I got sick of babysitting. I was twelve and I wanted to be out playing soccer. I took her to the park one Saturday and I guess I was bored and feeling mean. She was playing with her doll in the grass and she said, "Look. A bee." I said, "Catch it." I don't know why I said that; I didn't think she'd do it. She grabbed it in her hand to please me and, of course, she got stung. Just before she started to cry, she looked up at me, eyes large and shocked. Her hand was swelling and I ran cold water from the fountain over it. Her hand was so little and soft, and there was that angry red swelling. I rushed her home to our next-door neighbor and asked what to do. Mrs. Velez gave me meat tenderizer to put on it and she laughed at me because I was almost crying, too. "It's only a bee sting. Take it easy, it's no emergency."

Mercedes never told on me. I don't know if she remembers. She still looks up to me, and I'd never do anything to disappoint her trust.

I went into the bathroom and stood in the shower for a long time. I do my best thinking in private, with the water running over me. When she was younger, Mercedes used to dance in front of the TV right in everyone's way, doing a bad imitation of Madonna, and we'd have to yell at her to stop. Sometimes she'd get pesty, but that was from being so lively. She's at the head of sixth grade, straight A's, and her teacher even told Mama she's very, very bright. That's the way she said it, "very, *very* bright." Mercedes can take care of herself.

I scrubbed off the sweat and grime. I didn't want to think about the scene at the Delaneys'. Right, like trying not to think about a purple elephant. It was good I split before anything started.

When I came to school the next morning, John Masci was at the locker.

"How come you cut out?" he said. "I was looking for you."

I shrugged.

"Man, that was something else. You shoulda seen— You don't know what you missed! Hey, were you still there when Scott drilled her?"

"No. Scott—?" I was kind of curious.

"Yeah, we're all standing there, and Tim, the jerk, says to her, 'Who do you want?' " Masci was talking a mile a minute. "So she points to Scott. Rank on Bob, huh? Scott has her get down on all fours right there and he humps her from the back like a dog and we're all going 'De-lan-ey! De-lan-ey!' and she's squealing like anything." Masci's eyes were bright; he was all charged up. Wild horses couldn't have shut him up. "You know what Scott said? He's always wanted to try it like that. So then—"

I found my math text at the bottom of the locker. Well, a slut is a slut, no matter what. She asked for it.

"So then somebody says to break Tommy in, and Tommy's blushing like anything. We're going 'Go, Tommy!' and he can't get it up! He's like getting desperate and he grabs this miniature bottle off the shelf, you know, from Mr. D's collection, and he sticks it in and—"

"She let him do it with a *bottle?*" I said, incredulous. We started walking down the hall.

"She didn't say anything. Anyway, it was a Johnnie Walker miniature, not big enough to give her a charge—" Masci was laughing, excited. "Then it's like, who's next, and Clay says 'in size places'; he thinks he's superstud. But Dietrich fakes him out!"

It had snowballed out of control, I thought. Maybe Dietrich had the sense to stop it.

"Dietrich fakes him out and comes up with a mop handle from the kitchen!"

"Wait a minute," I said. "That's way over the line." I couldn't believe that *Bob Dietrich*, of all people . . . "That's sick."

"She wanted it. Hey, she loved it. She's thrashing and moaning and whimpering . . ." Some people passed us in the hall and Masci lowered his voice. "Then Scott's getting nervous about his mom coming home, so we hustle her out of there."

None of this has anything to do with me, I thought.

"But here's the best part. We're gonna have our own porn flick!"

"What?"

"We can get her to come back, no sweat. Our own X video! You and Charlie can get in it. You missed the—"

"Hey don't, you can't—," I said.

"Sure. Scott called that kid that lives next door, you know, Dan Gregory, the one with the camcorder? Scott was filling him in, said it was his golden opportunity to tape some great action. We were gonna do it this afternoon, but that kid's such a wuss, he said no."

"John—"

"Hey, we can find a camcorder someplace. We were making up titles, it was a panic."

"Shut up for a minute and listen to me," I said. He wasn't a mental giant, but he'd always been an OK guy. "Listen, stay out of it. The shit's gonna hit the fan."

"No way. She'll keep quiet."

"Listen to me. John, I'm talking to you like a friend. Don't do it."

"What's the matter with you?" he said. "We're having some fun, that's all."

CARA

THEY HURT ME.

I thought they were my friends.

I got scared. I saw the mop handle and I wanted my panties. They'd landed on a couch cushion when I was dancing, and I went to get them. They wouldn't let me put them on.

"You'll like it, Cara."

"Try it, you'll like it."

"The bigger the better."

"Come on, Cara, it'll be exciting."

Scott said I could get a date if I did it.

They pushed me down on the couch. Hands on my tits. Hands on my belly. Hands down there.

"Get some butter."

"What for, moron? You want a sandwich?"

"Put some butter on. Like in that movie."

"Come on, slide it in."

"Move over, I can't see!"

Faces above me. Faces everywhere. Faces staring down at me. I squinched my eyes shut tight.

They said it would be exciting. But it hurt. I wriggled to get away from it.

Then Scott told me to get cleaned up and go home because his mom might come back. No one looked at me. No one said anything. I got dressed.

Bob grabbed my shoulders and said, "You keep quiet, Cara."

He was holding my shoulders tight. "You're not going to blab, right, Cara?"

"Right," I said, and he let me go.

It was raining hard outside. I'm scared of lightning. I wanted to run, but I couldn't. I had to walk with little steps. There wasn't any thunder, but I was scared it would start. I'm scared of lightning. It was eleven blocks of little steps to get home. Lightning can hit you. You're not supposed to stand under a tree.

At home, the air-conditioning was on. It made goose bumps on my arms.

I heard Mommy talking on the telephone in the kitchen. I heard her say, "Oh, just a minute," and then she called, "Cara?"

"Yes."

"I looked for you at the track; I wanted to

give you a ride home. Did you get very wet?"

"Yes." The air-conditioning blowing on me made me shiver. "I'm taking a hot bath." I was so cold.

"OK, I'll be up in a minute. I'm sorry, my daughter just came in . . . You were talking about cutting the end of page six? I could make that cut, but then . . ."

I went upstairs to the bathroom. I got undressed. There was gunk on my panties. I threw everything in the hamper. It hurt to pee. I filled the tub. It hurt to lift my leg over the edge to get in. At first the water stung, but then it felt better. I sat in the warm water until my fingers got puckery.

Mommy knocked on the door. "Don't be too long, honey. Dinner's almost ready."

"OK."

After I dried off, I put lots of hand lotion on my finger and stuck it in my nookie. It burned! I didn't know what to do. It burned like anything! I sat down quick in the water that was left in the tub. It was cold. My teeth were chattering. I didn't know what to do.

I wanted my fuzzy old pajamas and they were way in the bottom of the drawer. I had to mess everything up to find them. I got into bed.

"Cara! Dinner's on the table!"

"I don't want any," I called.

I heard Mommy coming up the stairs. She came into my room. "What's the matter?" She sat down on the bed and felt my forehead. "Don't you feel well?"

I shook my head.

"You're white as a sheet."

"The lightning scared me so much."

"It's not a thunderstorm, pussycat." She stroked my hair back from my forehead. "Does something hurt?"

"No," I said fast.

"Do you feel like throwing up or—"

"No."

"—does your stomach hurt?"

"No! Stop talking! I'm tired. I want to go to sleep."

"All right." She stood up. "All right, I'll keep some chicken warm for you."

I was glad she went away because I wanted to tell her, but then she'd get mad and yell questions at me. Like the time with the bakery man.

It wasn't like the bakery man. They invited me to a party. Mommy doesn't know about the way it is in high school. Everyone hangs out in crowds, going to keg parties and stuff, having fun like on MTV. "Last night—what a blast . . ." Lots of girls fool around. I hear them talking. I'm not a retard; I'm friends with the popular guys.

I wasn't bad. I pointed at Scott 'cause Bob doesn't talk and Scott kids around with me and he's second most handsome. His eyes crinkle when he smiles. I don't know why they hurt me so much. I know it's bad to steal someone's boyfriend, but Laura Jean was snotty to me at the store.

I heard pots and dishes clattering in the kitchen; it sounded far away. It was lonely to be in bed when it was still daytime. I wanted my mommy! I scrunched into a little ball under my quilt. Just like Bunny's quilt. My favorite picture in *Bunny's Great Adventure* is the last one, when she's back in her den, all warm and cozy. Before that, she's on the hilltop, so tiny with all the trees and hills of the great wide world spread out before her. But then, she's back in her cozy den and I like to look at all the cute little things: The cupboard has jars of carrot jam and pickled carrots and carrot cookies. On the wall, there's a framed painting of lettuce and another of an old great-grandpa rabbit with glasses. They even have a special fox alarm to keep them safe. Bunny snuggles into her bed under a soft pink-

and-red quilt; Mommy painted it to look just like mine.

I have to go to school the next day. If I don't, Mommy will say I'm sick and take me to the doctor. After breakfast, I need to make but it hurts to push, so I hold it in.

I have lunch by myself in the fourth floor girls' room. Anne Pierce and those girls don't let me sit with them anymore. When there's an empty chair at their table, they say it's taken. Some girls come in to smoke and they say something about me eating in there. They look at me funny. I go into a stall and I don't come out until after they leave. I have a muffin. I throw most of it in the trash can because it makes me feel like I have to go to the bathroom and I'm afraid to.

After school, I have track practice. I change into my shorts with everybody else in the locker room. We always do warm-ups first. Mrs. Jensen isn't watching; she's talking to somebody. My stomach hurts. I don't do the stretches, but nobody sees. Then Mrs. Jensen says for us to do three laps.

It hurts. Even very slow, it hurts. It feels funny to stop right in the middle when everybody else is running. I sit down by myself on the bleachers. Mrs. Jensen sees me and comes over.

"What are you doing, Cara?"

"I can't run."

"Why not?"

"I don't feel well . . . I have my period."

She sighs. "All right, you can go on home."

"No," I say. "I'll watch." I want to be with everybody.

"OK," Mrs. Jensen says. She starts back to the track and then she stops and turns around. "Wait a minute." She sits down next to me. "What's this all about? You had your period last week—remember, you said you had cramps?"

"Oh."

"I know it's hot. It's just as hot for everyone else. I don't like phony excuses."

"I *can't* run."

"Cara?"

"It hurts," I whisper.

"What hurts?" She puts her arm around me. "What's wrong?"

I hide my face in her shoulder. All the crying in me explodes against her shoulder.

"All right, settle down." She strokes my back. "All right now, settle down. Tell me what's wrong."

I tell her.

"I'm sorry, Cara. Your mother has to know."

"No, Mrs. Jensen. Please, don't tell."

"I'm sorry. I have to."

She won't listen to me, no matter what I say. She gives Helene her stopwatch and tells her to handle the rest of practice. She makes me get into her car and she drives me home. I go straight upstairs to my room, but I can hear them in the living room. They're talking about me. I curl up in a ball on the bed. I can hear them. Mommy's voice sounds bad. Then Mrs. Jensen calls me down. I don't want to come downstairs.

"Cara!" Mrs. Jensen calls again.

I'm scared. I come into the living room. Mommy is sitting bent over on the couch with her face in her hands.

Mrs. Jensen has a notebook and a pencil. "Cara, give me all their names. Everyone who was there."

"No, I don't—"

Mommy looks up. Her hand is pressed against her throat.

"I don't want to talk about it anymore," I say. "Please, Mommy . . ."

"The boys who . . . did this . . . to you. Their names." Mommy's words come squeezed out with big spaces in between.

Mrs. Jensen says, "You told me Scott Delaney and Bob Dietrich. Scott and Bob and . . . Come on, Cara, who else?"

I'm scared. "Tommy Delaney," I say. "And—*uh*—Mike Clay."

Mrs. Jensen is writing. "Go on. And—?"

I'm going to be in big trouble. "Can't we just forget about it?"

"No," Mommy says. "Go on."

There were all the faces staring down at me. All the faces. "There were some I don't know their names . . . Tim . . . I don't know." I start to cry. "There were a lot."

Mommy reaches for me and pulls me down to the couch next to her. She holds me against her and rocks me.

"It's all right, Cara," Mrs. Jensen says. "Tell me the ones you do know."

I get confused. I close my eyes and I see them sitting around the lunch table, kidding around and stuff. "John Masci. Charlie Goren. Joe Lopez. Mike Clay."

Mrs. Jensen and Mommy are ganging up on me, waiting for me to say more.

"A redhead boy with freckles . . . I don't know all the names."

"Ellen, do you want me to call the police?

And she should have medical— I *know* those boys, it's hard to believe they—"

"No, don't." I'm crying. "No police. Please, no police."

"The doctor first," Mommy says. "I want our own doctor."

"Ellen, can I drive you—?"

Mommy shakes her head.

"Is there anything I can do? Anything at all?"

Mommy keeps shaking her head.

"They're all Shorehaven students." Mrs. Jensen sighs. "I'll report it to Mr. Gilmartin."

I can feel Mommy's whole body shaking.

"I don't want to go to Dr. Crane." I don't want to tell him, too. I don't want to keep telling.

"Buckle your seat belt." Mommy's voice is hollow, like a robot's.

"I don't need the doctor, Mommy, I don't want to—"

She turns on the ignition. She stares straight ahead through the windshield. Her lips are pressed together so tight; there's a white line all around them.

She drives to the end of the driveway and

then she brakes so suddenly that I bounce forward.

"Where are they?"

"What?"

"Those boys. Where are they now?"

"I don't know." She's making me cry. "The baseball field?"

She drives very fast and the car jerks at the Stop sign. She's driving like she's mad at the car. Tears are running down her face. I don't think she knows because she doesn't wipe them away. They make long shiny lines on her face.

"We're finding them!" she says.

There's no one at the ball field. She circles around it. Then she stops and bangs on the wheel with her fist. "Where are they? Cara! Where?"

She's scaring me. "Maybe—Baskin-Robbins?"

I don't want to get my friends in trouble.

She makes a U-turn and the tires squeal. She drives fast down the Boulevard. She hits the brakes across the street from Baskin-Robbins. The car shudders. There are a whole lot of kids outside.

"Is that them?" She stares out the window. Her body is stiff.

There are a whole lot of kids. I see a jacket something like John Masci's, I'm not sure. I don't see anyone else.

"Is it?"

"No." She's scaring me and making me cry. "Mommy? What are you going to do, Mommy?"

For the first time, she turns and looks at me. Her mouth opens, but she doesn't say anything. She just looks at me. Then her shoulders sag and her arms collapse down on the steering wheel. "I don't know," she whispers. She hits the horn by mistake; it blares and she jerks up.

"I wanted to run them down," she whispers. "My God! I was going to run them down!"

LAURA JEAN

THERE WAS SOMETHING PECULIAR GOING ON AT school.

In the morning, I saw John Masci in the hall, in the middle of a big knot of guys—Mike Clay, Tim Hughes, and some of those younger ones. They were laughing and talking up a storm. I went over and I swear I saw Masci nudging somebody and all of a sudden the conversation stopped dead.

"Hi," I said.

"Oh. Hi, L.J.," Masci said. He had the strangest look on his face, like he'd been caught with his hand in the cookie jar. They were all standing there, looking at me.

"What are you guys up to?"

"Nothing much," Clay mumbled, and I swear that kid Greeley started giggling. I hate it when *girls* giggle, but on a boy, it's the pits. I felt like they didn't want me around, so I said, "See you," and kept on going.

I wondered if they'd been talking about *me*. I walked down the hall feeling uncomfortable and left out. That was silly; I'm in the group and the guys wouldn't turn on me, but . . . I just couldn't help wondering what they'd been saying that I wasn't supposed to hear.

Then, in the middle of animal science, Mr. Held got a call on the intercom and told Masci and Dietrich they were wanted in the main office.

After class, I went up to the third floor to catch Scott on his way out of English. He wasn't with the kids streaming out of 310. I saw Sue Franklin and I said, "I guess I just missed him, huh?" and I kind of laughed because sometimes Scott is out of a classroom like a shot.

"He's not here," Sue said. "He was called down to the main office right in the middle of class."

"The main office? Do you know why?"

She shrugged. "Search me."

The main office. The school secretary and the attendance office. And Mr. Gilmartin's office. Masci and Dietrich, and Scott, too. I wondered what that was all about. Maybe they had to fill out some athletic forms . . . But right in the middle of class? There was something peculiar going on.

JOE LOPEZ

"So you can see that the Louisiana Purchase had an immediate—" The intercom buzzed. Mrs. Hadley tried to finish the sentence. "—an immediate impact on America because—" It buzzed again, and she sighed with frustration. While she answered, I examined my ballpoint. It was leaving ink stains on my fingers. I hate when that happens.

"Joe Lopez. They want you in the main office."

I was startled. "Now?"

"Yes, they said immediately."

Leave my books? Take them? I picked them up automatically while my blood drained down to my shoes. An emergency. Mercedes. An accident at the elementary school.

The hall was empty and silent, a passage of closed classroom doors. I took the stairs two at a time. Last winter, Larry Reise was called out in the middle of physics; his mother had been killed in a collision on Shore Road. Right in the middle of the morning, on her way home from Pathmark. Please not Mama, Mercedes, Dolores, Gloria. I caught my breath in front of the door to the main office. Mercedes. One last moment left before I found out the worst. Please, God, I'll do anything . . . My hand cramped on the doorknob as I turned it.

Scott, Bob, Masci, Charlie Goren, and Mike Clay were in the reception area. *¡Gracias a Dios!* It was something else!

I felt light-headed. I pulled myself together. "What's happening?"

"Gilmartin wants to see us," Masci mumbled.

I went to the secretary at the desk. "I'm Joe Lopez." My lips felt stiff.

"OK." She checked a list. "We're waiting for two more."

About Cara Snowden, I thought.

The guys were huddled together, talking low. I went over. "Who're they waiting for?"

"My brother and Tim Hughes," Scott said.

"Anybody know why?" I asked.

Bob looked grim. "You think Cara . . . ? Hell no, she wouldn't . . ."

"What do we say?" Masci asked.

"Listen, we tell the truth, that's all." Scott shrugged, cool, but he was cracking his knuckles. "She wanted it, so we accommodated her. What, is there a law against that?"

"Yeah," Masci said. "It's none of The Munchkin's business, anyway."

"Keep it down." Bob nodded toward the secretary.

Good thing I cut out, I thought.

"Wait a minute," Charlie said. "It's not about her. I wasn't even there."

"Hey, that's right!" Masci looked relieved. "All right!"

Asshole, I thought, *I told you . . .*

Tommy came in and then Tim Hughes, out of breath, a little while after. "I got called out of gym!"

We waited, not saying much. They were looking around at each other. I avoided the glances; I wasn't part of this. We were ushered into Mr. Gilmartin's office. Chairs scraped, shoes shuffled against the floor. There weren't enough chairs for everybody. Scott, Tim, and I stood.

Mr. Gilmartin was standing at the window, his back to us. The tick of his desk clock was the only sound. Finally, he turned and faced us, his hands spread wide and gripping the edge of the desk. He cleared his throat. "There's been a serious complaint—*uh*—serious accusation. Mrs. Jensen gave me this list this morning, and I have to tell you, it made me sick to see your names. You boys, of all people—athletes and leaders—"

Crack. Scott's knuckles.

"What are we being accused of?" Bob was stony-faced.

Mr. Gilmartin cleared his throat again. "Gang rape," he spit out. "Abusing Cara Snowden. A student at this school. A retarded girl."

"There was no rape," Scott burst out. "She's lying!"

And then everyone was talking at once. "She followed us around all the time! We couldn't get rid of her."

"She wanted it! She was begging for it!"

I didn't do it, and I wasn't going to go down for it. "She gave you my name? I left before—," I started.

Mr. Gilmartin interrupted. "According to Mrs. Jensen, you lured Cara to the Delaneys' house and—"

"*Lured?* She invited herself, we didn't want her there," Bob said. "And then she went and did a striptease in front of—"

Gilmartin waved Bob away. "I don't want to hear it."

Crack.

"Would you stop that!" He was furious.

"Sorry, sir," Scott mumbled. "I didn't know I was doing it."

"How does Mrs. Jensen come into this?" Clay said.

"The girl reported it to her." Mr. Gilmartin was red-faced. "A bottle. *Uh*—a mop handle!"

"Wait a minute, it was a *miniature*. A tiny, little Johnnie Walker miniature."

"Hey, she was willing, that's the truth! She wanted to try something new . . . She was looking for kicks."

"She's lying," Charlie Goren said, "because I wasn't even there. I can prove I went straight home and if anything goes on my record, my dad's gonna be down here suing the pants off this school." Charlie's dad is a hotshot New York lawyer.

Mr. Gilmartin swung around and looked at him. "Don't bother to tell me your story, it's out of my jurisdiction. It wasn't on school time or on school property, so it's not *my* responsibility. It's a police matter. I'm passing it on to the police."

I looked for an opening to say I'd left, but he had just cut Charlie off.

"Do you have to tell the police?" John Masci looked uncomfortable. "There wasn't a crime."

"You'll see what your father thinks about that," Mr. Gilmartin said. "What disgusts me— not that I condone your initial lapse of judgment, getting carried away is no excuse—but what really disgusts me is your planning to go on with it. A *premeditated taping!*"

Scott's eyebrows shot up. Glances were exchanged.

"That's all. I truly pray the police investigation shows there's been some mistake. Maybe you weren't all involved." His glance lingered on Bob Dietrich. "I hope not. But I'm telling you right now, you'd better keep your noses clean. Around this school, for the rest of the term, you'd better be above reproach. One infraction, any little thing, and you're suspended." He punctuated his words with a pointing finger. "Got that?"

"Mr. Gilmartin," I started, "I wasn't—"

"Now get out!" He paced to the window and turned his back to us. "Just get out!"

The whole session in his office took no more

than five minutes. He seemed in a big rush to get us off his hands.

We left the main office. In the hall, Mike Clay started to talk and Scott nudged him and put his finger over his lips. We waited until we got to the stairwell, well out of earshot. Then Bob exploded with "The lying bitch!"

"She must be crazy! She spreads her legs and goes and broadcasts it!"

"Jeeze! I never thought she'd talk."

"I didn't touch her," Tim said. "I never touched her."

"Yeah, right."

"I didn't! I was just watching . . ."

I stood apart. *Had anyone seen me leave? How in hell was I going to prove it?*

"You had to get a friggin' mop!" Clay said to Bob. "Why'd you have to get the friggin' mop!"

"Shut your mouth!" Bob glared at him. "You were doing plenty, I saw you . . ."

"Hey, cut it out," Goren said. "You guys got in it together, you better figure a way out together."

Long silence. Eyes darted around.

Tommy Delaney looked scared. He kept looking over at Scott. Scott studied the floor.

"What's going to happen?" Tim asked. No one answered.

"Wait, she didn't know about the taping," Scott said. "How did he find out about the taping?"

"Anybody pass it on?" Bob said.

"I told Joe and Charlie," John Masci said. "That's all."

A couple of glances my way.

"Yeah, I told Charlie, too," Clay said.

"Anybody else? Hughes, you talk to anybody?"

"No. Not me."

"Tommy?"

"No way."

"Who else but us—?"

There was a silence.

"Dan Gregory. It had to be Gregory," Tommy said.

"Not Dan. Shit, I can't believe—"

"It had to be, Scott."

"It must've been him. Remember, you said he acted weird about it?"

"Shit!" Scott punched his fist into his hand. "The fink sonofabitch!"

"Oh man, he'll get his," Clay said.

"Chill," Bob said. "We got to keep a low profile."

"Are we supposed to go back to class now?" Tim asked.

"What for? The period's almost over."

"Yeah, but he said 'above reproach' . . ."

"Don't sweat it. Gilmartin's not gonna do anything."

Scott cleared his throat and went into a pretty good imitation. "A bottle. *Uh*—a mop handle!"

"Yeah, he wants his old lady to try it," Clay said.

"They didn't get Greeley or Jimbo. How the hell did they stay off the list?"

"If this messes up my scholarship . . . ," Scott muttered.

Tim Hughes looked about to wet his pants. "What's the police going to do?"

"Don't worry, we've got an in with the mayor." Scott winked at Masci. "Piece of cake." Pause. "Right, Masci?"

Masci couldn't muster a smile.

Why did she have to name *me*? I could get screwed over. For nothing. For nothing!

The others were trying to laugh it off, but there were giveaways: a muscle twitching in Bob's cheek, Masci's drawn face. The only one who wasn't uptight was Charlie Goren.

LAURA JEAN

By THAT AFTERNOON, IT WAS ALL OVER THE SCHOOL that Cara Snowden got the boys in trouble.

Some of the guys from the wrestling team were laughing at the lockers: "Cara did a striptease." "Hell, we shoulda been there!" "The Delaneys and Dietrich . . ."

I kept hearing Scott's name. I was hearing bits and pieces all afternoon. I couldn't help putting them together.

A knot of girls had gathered in front of the library: "When her mother found out, she cried rape." "She pointed right at Scott, she asked for it." "The boys are so pissed . . ."

Scott's name again. I wanted to know and I didn't want to know. I was friendly with those girls. I could have gone over and asked. But I didn't want to be told in public, with everyone watching my face.

I went through my classes automatically. I

wrapped myself in a bubble of isolation. Plastic bubble wrap from head to toe.

I didn't see him until school let out. He was waiting for me on the front steps.

"L.J.!"

"Hi." I went over. I felt stiff and awkward with him. It felt like back at the very beginning, in seventh grade, groping for something to say.

"Are you working this afternoon?" he said.

"No."

"Oh, right."

Pause.

"*Uh*—don't you have practice?"

"No, it's been canceled."

"Oh."

He looked at me. I looked at him. He was fidgety.

Finally, I said, "We have to talk."

"OK, go ahead and talk. What about?"

"You tell me what about," I said.

"What do you mean?"

"It's all over the school, you know! I'm not deaf, dumb, and blind!"

"What? What did you hear?"

"I don't know," I said. "You tell me."

"What? I'm not playing guessing games."

I was afraid my expression would crumble. "We have to talk someplace private."

We started aimlessly down the stairs.

"The woods?" I said.

"OK."

We went around to the back of the school. We followed the dirt path past the baseball field.

"Do we have to go in perfect silence?" he said. "Like, are we allowed to say a few words on the way?"

I felt him studying me, trying to make me smile.

"How about this weather?" he said. "Hey, how about those Mets?"

I was ice.

We went through the trees. The path was moldy with old leaves. We were in dappled shade. The only sound was the faint rustle of the undergrowth as we brushed past it. The silence between us spread and spread.

Finally, I stopped. I tore a leaf off a branch. It was small and pale green. I concentrated on its veins.

"Did you gang rape Cara Snowden?" I blurted.

"What? Are you crazy?"

I looked up.

"I'm not a *rapist!* That's one hell of a thing to say!"

"I meant, did the guys—did *somebody* gang rape her?"

"Did I ever—back when you had me climbing the walls—did I ever try to *force* you? When you said no, did I respect it? Well, answer me, did I?"

I nodded.

"So where did that come from?"

"Maybe you'd better tell me. Because I've been hearing things all day."

"I swear to you, I swear on my mother's life, Cara never said no. Nobody was threatening her. What do you think—we had knives and guns? She wanted to. She let us do anything we wanted."

"*Us?* You, too?"

"I'll tell you how it happened."

"Go ahead."

"Look, I'm sorry you had to hear about it. It had nothing to do with you. It didn't mean a thing."

"Don't make excuses. Just tell me."

There was a cracking noise behind us. It might have been a squirrel.

"Do you know Cara Snowden?" he said.

"No, not really."

"She's a whore. She's been doing everybody in school."

"You, too?"

"No, not me. She had a crush on Bob Dietrich, so she's been following us around. It was a joke. Every place we went, lunch and everything. Monday afternoon, we're hanging at the ball field and—"

"Monday? The day I took Janice's shift."

"Yeah. Well, she trots right over. We're talking about going over to my house and she follows us in."

"She follows you in," I said, "and you couldn't pry her away. Scott, I'm not stupid."

"The next thing you know, she takes off all her clothes. I swear to God, she takes them off on her own, by herself. She's standing there naked in front of ten guys, waiting. So what would you expect?"

"Scott—"

"It happens. Remember when I went to check out Dartmouth? Remember I was invited to that frat party? Tau something. Some girl got drunk and was up in a room, and all night long I saw different guys heading up to that room. It happens. In the Ivies, too."

"Did *you* have sex with her?"

"The girl at the frat? No."

"Cara." I felt on the edge of a nightmare. "I'll hear about it anyway."

"You're making a mountain out of—"

"Say yes or no." *Please let him say no,* I prayed, *and I'll make myself believe him.*

He hesitated, too long. All I could see was the bark of a tree, all the lines and grooves jumping out at me.

"Yes or no." My lips were numb.

"Yes, but—"

" 'L.J. and Scott, Eternal Love'!" I tugged blindly at the clasp of my bracelet until it came loose. "That was some eternal love!" I pitched it into the bushes; I heard the heart clink as it hit something. I started to run down the path, but Scott caught my arm and whirled me back.

"Let go! You're hurting me!"

"What did you do that for?"

"What did I do that for?" I repeated incredulously.

"You wanted to know what happened! So stay and listen! She's standing naked, waiting for it, and one of the guys, says, 'Who do you want?' She points at me. What do you expect me to do in front of all the guys? You expect me to say, 'No thanks'? It wasn't anything personal. It was like all of us, doing it together."

"You didn't have to—"

"It was wham, bam, that's it. I wasn't *cheating* on you. There's a difference between humping and making love."

"And I'd never have to know?"

"That's right. It didn't matter."

"Great! Terrific! And then you'd come back to me and maybe bring me a disease and—"

"Jeeze, I never thought of that."

"I've never been with anyone else."

"I know that . . . I *love* you, L.J. I'd cut off my right arm before I'd hurt you."

"Then I don't understand why you'd want—" I trailed off into a whisper.

"Cara's into kinky stuff, things I'd never in a million years ask you to do, and—Christ, she was willing to try it with—you know those little bottles my dad collects?"

I winced. I didn't want to imagine . . .

"Like a porn flick come to life. It was crazy and exciting, and kind of funny. Guys get turned on, they get carried away . . . I know, I was stupid, I'm no saint, but it had nothing to do with you."

"She was exciting; that has everything to do with me."

"*She* wasn't. The—situation was."

"So long, Scott. I have nothing to say to you."

I was ice cold. I wasn't going to break. I was poised to walk away.

"Don't do that to me, L.J. Not now."

I'd always loved the dark leaf-mold smell of the woods, but now I couldn't smell anything. My senses had shut down. I couldn't move.

"L.J. I'm in real trouble," Scott said. He'd dropped his cool; I'd never seen him look so vulnerable.

I resisted, I really resisted feeling anything.

"Gilmartin's reporting it to the police."

I shrugged with the most indifference I could manage.

"I don't know what's going on in Cara's mind—maybe somebody found out, maybe she got scared, so she's yelling rape. She's crucifying us for nothing. Maybe she wants attention."

"The police?"

"Gilmartin's such an asshole. It's none of his business!" Scott was chewing at his lip. "It was one of those things. A dumb mistake. I can't undo it, so now I'm stuck in it, knee deep in it."

She was so pushy that day at Foodtown, almost grabbing at me. This—this *nobody* was destroying everything, for me, for Scott, for all of us. I was rigid with hating her.

"The Shorehaven police?" I said.

"I guess."

"Isn't Masci's dad— Isn't the mayor over the police? So it should be OK."

"I don't know. It could mess me up with Dartmouth. Who knows what happens next? I'm walking around waiting for the other shoe to drop."

He had picked up a branch and was methodically stripping it.

"My folks are gonna know. God, my mom, even Ginny . . . They'll blame me for dragging Tommy into it."

"You're not responsible for—"

"He follows me. It's always been like that. They'll say it's my fault."

When there's trouble, it can either split people apart or draw them together. That time when I had the false alarm—I was sure I was pregnant. I was terrified and Scott was great. He said we'd handle it any way I wanted. I know a lot of boys walk when that happens, but Scott was there for me, all the way. He was great. It was almost nice in a way, the two of us together, against the world.

"Don't worry," I said. "She's lying and all of you are witnesses."

"Witnesses for each other; that won't mean

much." He threw the branch on the ground. "She could be saying anything. If she makes it stick—people go to jail for rape."

"No, that's not possible, not you and Dietrich and—"

"Right, public enemy number one." His laugh was short and harsh. He slouched, hands deep in his jeans pockets, and stared off into space. "Yeah, it'll blow over. They're not going to mess with Masci."

"She's lying, so it has to be OK," I said.

"Thanks."

"For what?"

"Just—thanks." He gave me a ghost of that crooked smile.

"I'm sorry," he said. He reached for my hand and I let him hold it.

"I want you to know," Scott said, tracing lines on my palm, "I thought very hard about what to put on that heart. They couldn't fit more than twelve letters on each side. 'L.J. and Scott, Eternal Love.' I meant that. Every word."

"My bracelet!" I touched the bareness of my wrist.

"Come on, I'll help you find it." Scott worked a path through the trees, pushing boughs out of the way. "Around here?"

"No. I don't know." I went through the underbrush. I tried to remember where I'd heard it clink. Gold would shine. But there was nothing. Branches scraped against my arms. "It could be anywhere."

"Yeah, you've got a great arm," he called.

I could have *handed* it back to him, no matter what. He'd picked it out for me, he'd carefully chosen the right words, and I threw it away! I sank to my knees and felt around in the leaves and moss.

"This far back?"

"I don't know." I scrambled frantically over rocks and soil. There were ants and beetles and rotting logs. Prickly bushes tugged at my shirt.

I searched and searched. A thorn scratched my forehead; it stung and made my eyes water. I couldn't wipe them; my hands were covered with mud. I was going in circles. I knew it was hopeless. And finally I sat down.

"It's gone. I've lost it."

Scott was moving dead leaves with his foot. "I'm gonna get it for you. It's got to be someplace."

I sat on the ground and felt the dampness seep through my jeans. I heard him thrashing through the bushes.

"It's no use," I said. "We might as well go."

"No. I'm not quitting."

I knew how stubborn Scott could get. I watched him searching between the trees, bending, checking the ground, straightening up, going on, and I felt so bad for him. I ached for both of us.

"Scott, it's gone."

"No. I'm finding it for you." Then he went into deep shade and I couldn't see him anymore. All I could hear was the rustling of leaves. I put my arms around my knees and rested my head on them.

"L.J.!"

I stood up.

He came leaping back, crashing through bushes, dangling the heart on his finger. "You know where it was? It got caught on a branch! It never hit the ground!"

He tentatively held it out toward me.

I hesitated. So he wasn't perfect. I stretched out my arm and gave him my wrist. I studied the familiar planes of his face as he bent over the clasp. His face was so solemn and I wanted to touch it. He needed me.

JOE LOPEZ

JOHN MASCI SHOWED UP FOR SCHOOL THE NEXT day with a split lip and a huge blue bruise extending past his T-shirt sleeve.

"Jeeze, what happened to you?" I said.

"You should see my back. My old man beat the shit out of me. Sonofabitch!"

I didn't know if that was for his father or Gilmartin. Whatever, it had been reported to the police.

The guys were crowding around. "What's he going to do? What did he say?"

"Like I embarrassed him." Masci talked out of the side of his mouth, touching it with his hand. "Like how could I be dumb enough to go in my own backyard. He went at me with his belt!"

Maybe having a father ain't all that it's cracked up to be, I thought. If anybody tried that on me, I wouldn't stand still and take it.

"Yeah, but what's he going to *do*?"

"Nothing. He's not interfering. Man, he was pissed! He's having Schroeder and Allen handle it."

Schroeder and Allen, the Keystone Kops, big on busting kids drinking beer on the field at night.

On and off through the day, we were talking about it. I sat with them at lunch. I had to know what was coming down.

"Schroeder and Allen won't do nothing," Clay said. "You think they're gonna bust the mayor's son?"

Scott looked worried. "Masci says they're coming around to all our houses tonight. Starting the investigation."

"Well, my dad's getting some affadavits together." Charlie Goren laughed. "Affadavits from eight Episcopalian ladies."

"What?"

"My mom's on the bazaar committee. They were over at my house when I came home. At three-thirty. I politely said hello to them before I went upstairs. So, hey, I've only got eight church-lady witnesses . . ."

"Charlie—you think we need lawyers?"

"Can't hurt."

A knot was in my stomach. Where was I supposed to get a lawyer?

All day long, I was picturing the scenario. Schroeder coming up to the apartment, Mama not understanding and scared by the *policía*. Hey, Ma, we're not in Salvador anymore, it's the U.S. of A. But she's bowing and scraping to show respect, terrified of Authority, with a capital A. Teachers, civil service clerks, most of all *policía!* I had to get her out of the apartment some way tonight.

OK, Mama's out and Schroeder comes in, a big redneck guy toting a .38.

"Hey, man," I say, "I was gone before anything happened. I cut out."

"Oh yeah? When was this?"

"About four."

"You're telling me you passed? You expect me to believe that?" His eyes are saying "spic."

My hands ball into fists. I'm going to slam him.

"Where do you *say* you went?"

"Straight home."

"Sure. Anybody see you on the street?"

"No. Look, it was pouring. Nobody was out."

"Nobody saw you, huh? You were home about four?"

"Four-fifteen, four-thirty by the time I got there."

"Any witnesses?"

"No," I say.

"Where was your mother?"

"Working."

"Oh? What does she do?"

"Cleans up other people's dirt," I snarl.

"You're a surly bastard, right? You've got three sisters. And nobody's home to see you. Convenient. You were the one with the mop, weren't you?"

"No! I left! Listen, my kid sister was here. But she's only eleven."

"All right, I'll talk to her."

"No. No way. Leave her out of this."

I bar his way, but he shoves me aside. Mercedes is in tears. He grins at me, gap between his teeth. "She's lying for you. Doesn't mean a thing."

Along with rape, I'm going to get assault on an officer.

That was my scenario. The way it happened that night was completely different.

Mama was home. I was right about one part— her eyes getting big and dark with terror.

"Sorry to disturb you, Mrs. Lopez," Schroeder

said. He was wearing a regular suit and he smelled of cologne. "I need to ask your son a couple of questions." He looked around the apartment. "Anyplace we can talk privately?"

I led him into the kitchen. I could smell my own fear, and I hated it. We sat down at the table.

"I ought to have a lawyer here," I said. "All I'm gonna say is I left before anything happened. I left and went straight home and that's the truth. That's all I have to say."

"Take it easy, son." Schroeder smiled. "There's no need to read you the Miranda."

"What?"

"We know you left, Joe. Bob Dietrich saw you go. And John Masci told us."

I exhaled a breath I didn't know I was holding. Masci and Dietrich, OK guys. I owed them.

"You were a witness, and I'm trying to get a handle on exactly what took place. You weren't directly involved, you have no ax to grind— Just tell me what happened, what you saw, up to the time you left, in your own words."

I told him, straight and factual. He asked a couple of questions: Did anyone force her into the Delaneys' house? Did anyone tear her clothes off? No to both. Everything you saw was voluntary on her part? Yes.

"If it ever reached that point, would you be able to testify to that under oath?"

"Yeah, sure," I said.

"Thanks for your time, Joe." And on his way out, "Sorry to interrupt your evening, Mrs. Lopez."

I had all these good feelings for Dietrich and Masci; they came through for me. Maybe not for *me*. Maybe because I could be a friendly witness. No difference. It was over.

CARA

SOME BOYS, I DON'T KNOW THEIR NAMES, CALLED me in the hall at school. They called, "Cara! You want some Scotch? You like Johnnie Walker, right?"

This afternoon, a bunch of girls were pointing at me and laughing and they said, "Where's your mop?"

I don't mind that much. I just don't listen to them. I don't mind that much. When the kids called me "dummy" in second grade, Mommy said not to listen. Sticks and stones can break my bones, but names will never hurt me.

I wasn't supposed to tell. I only told Mrs. Jensen and I didn't even mean to. No one likes me anymore. I said "hi" to Bob Dietrich and he said "bitch" to me.

I don't want to go to school anymore, but Mommy makes me. She says it's almost the end of the year and I've been doing well and she won't let anything stop me now. She's always acting like my big boss.

I *told* her I wouldn't talk to the policeman tonight. I hear him come in. I hear them talking and then Mommy calls, "Cara!"

I keep the door of my room shut and I put my hands over my ears.

"Cara!"

She comes upstairs to get me.

"Go away! Make him go away!"

"It's OK, sweetie. I'll be there with you. All you have to do is tell what happened. One more time."

"The last time? Promise, the very last time?"

"I don't know," Mommy says, "but you have to come downstairs. Please, Cara."

He's sitting in the chair across from the couch. Mommy makes me sit down on the couch next to her. He says his name is Bill Schroeder. He smells like my daddy's after-shave, but he's looking at me funny.

"Why don't you tell me what happened, Cara, in your own words?" he says.

I don't know what words he means. I look at the red and blue squares on the carpet and I say it fast. "Scott did me from the back and then Tommy was going to, but he took the little bottle and they were all watching and yelling stuff and they did it with the mop and it hurt and then I went home."

"Cara, did you *invite* Scott Delaney to—*uh*—perform the act?"

He's looking at me funny and I'm scared. "No!" I say. "No!"

"She was *raped!*" Mommy says.

"Why don't we start at the beginning," he says. "How did you happen to be in the Delaneys' house?"

"They said I could come with them." The red squares are bigger than the blue squares. There are lines in between.

He has a notebook and a gold pen. "You went voluntarily?"

I don't know what to say.

"No one forced you to go, is that right?"

"I thought there was a party."

"Cara, did you—*uh*—do a striptease? Take your clothes off by yourself? In front of all the boys?"

Mommy is listening. I'm scared. I say, "No."

"Of course she didn't!" Mommy says. "What kind of question—"

"Mrs. Snowden, I'm sorry, but there's a witness who says she did."

"For God's sake, can't you see she's a *child?*"

"Cara, you said Charlie Goren was one of the boys who—abused—you."

"Uh-huh."

He sighs. "Mrs. Snowden, Charlie Goren was definitely not present. He was in his own home that afternoon, and there was a committee of the Episcopalian Sisterhood . . . They all saw him at home."

"Cara?" Mommy says.

"I don't remember." I can't remember all the faces. Bob and Scott and Tommy and Mike Clay and John Masci and . . . Charlie at the lunch table. I did Charlie in the auditorium balcony. I look at Mommy. "Maybe I made a mistake," I say.

"It's all right," he says. "We all make mistakes sometimes."

I want to suck my thumb, but I'm not supposed to. I bite my thumbnail instead.

He clears his throat. "Mrs. Snowden, there was that accusation a few years ago. The records are sealed, but you can't tell what a lawyer will drag up. Are you sure you want to put her through that? Are you sure you want to press charges again?"

"My daughter was gang raped!"

"Cara will be questioned and—"

"No more! I don't want any more questions!" My stomach feels bad and I almost cry. "Mommy, you promised, no more!"

"—and there are some inconsistencies. She named a boy who wasn't there at all. And it seems that she did have relations with some of these boys before."

"That can't be!" Mommy says. "She doesn't date!"

"I'm sorry, it seems there have been—incidents—around the school. There are witnesses. These are things that would come up . . ."

He turns the top of his gold pen around and around.

"It's your decision, of course. Frankly, if it was my daughter . . ."

I don't know what he means. I don't know what he's going to do. I chew on my thumbnail.

I hear Mommy whisper, "Oh, God."

He keeps turning the top of his pen.

There is a long silence. I hear Mommy breathing.

His notebook is on his lap. He didn't write in it.

The couch creaks.

"Nothing happened." Mommy's voice sounds dead and I look at her. Her face is blank. "Nothing at all. Forget it."

He nods.

"Cara, you can go upstairs now," Mommy says in the dead voice. "There'll be no more questions."

I run up to my room, and I close the door. I cross my arms over my chest and I hug myself.

LAURA JEAN

I DREADED SCHOOL THE NEXT DAY BECAUSE I thought I'd feel humiliated, but it wasn't like that. Girls I hardly even knew were going out of their way to be nice to me. "It's so rotten the way that skank got them in trouble" and "Don't worry, Laura Jean, it'll blow over. Scott will be OK." I was getting too much sympathy from people who weren't my friends. I mean, it was nice of them, but it made me uncomfortable.

It was all over the school and it seemed like everyone was behind the guys one hundred percent. I heard some of the younger second-string athletes talking. They'd caught Dan Gregory on his way to school that morning; someone said his nose got broken. "Serves him right for finking." "Yeah, we creamed that snitch!" *Dan Gregory?* What did *he* do? He was nice that day in the sin bin.

I wanted to skip the cafeteria scene, so Pat

and I cut out and had lunch at the pizzeria. We were sitting in a booth in the back, as far as we could get from the noise of the video games.

"I wish *somebody* liked anchovy pizza," I said. "I can never get anyone to share."

Pat said, "You mean Scott won't eat anchovies for you?" The edge to her voice startled me.

We wound up ordering pepperoni, and we were just talking in general. I was drinking my Coke, when she suddenly said, "So Scott doesn't tell you everything after all, does he?"

I sat up straight. That came right from the conversation we'd had on the way to Lord & Taylor's. I couldn't believe that she would bring it up now.

"He told me all about what happened," I mumbled.

"Right, after you found out," she said.

I pushed the Coke away. I looked at her; I couldn't say a word.

"Sorry, L.J., but—"

"Sorry?"

"—but now you know how it feels."

"What?"

"It was so easy for you to trash *my* boyfriend. Every chance you got."

"No, wait a minute. I'd find you crying because he put you down and— Well, all those times he canceled at the last minute and— You said yourself, he calls you an airhead and—"

"OK, he gets irritable; he has such a big vocabulary and sometimes I mispronounce things—but you can't imagine how nice he is to me sometimes and—"

"No, I can't imagine."

"You're so smug, Laura Jean."

"No, I was thinking about *you*. Ron Gilbert's on a power trip and he's got you so—"

"Scott Delaney is perfect. No matter what he does, he comes up smelling like roses."

"Look, this is bad enough without you—"

"Don't worry, everybody's backing the jocks. A bunch of wanna-bes kicked Dan Gregory's ass this morning. Hey, what's a little rape between friends?"

I looked at Pat and I was seeing a whole different person. I wanted to leave. I took out some bills and dropped them on the table. "That should be enough," I said icily.

"L.J., wait—I'm sorry, I—"

"I don't think I want to hear anything else from you," I said.

"Look, I'm sorry, I don't know why I said—"

I was blindly gathering my books. "There wasn't any rape," I said.

"L.J., I'm sorry, I swear to God. I don't know

what gets into me." She grabbed my hand. "Come on, stay. We've been friends too long for—"

"Some friend. You're the only one that's made a dig at me. The only one. Everyone's saying it was all that girl's fault. You *know* Scott. You know he wouldn't hurt a fly."

She tightened her grip. "I didn't mean it."

"They're regular guys, good guys, you *know* them. Maybe Mike Clay, but not the rest of them."

"I know." Pat cleared her throat. "Scott loves you, he really does, everyone knows that, and I wish— Maybe sometimes I get kind of jealous, I don't want to, but— I guess I wish I could feel that sure of someone. I'd never hurt you on purpose. I wouldn't."

I sank back into my seat.

"I'd do anything to help you through this—," she said.

The pizza came. We concentrated on tearing apart the slices.

"—because you're my best friend, L.J. Just about all my best memories are with you. Remember all the fun we had when we were little? We weren't scared of anyone or anything. Sledding down Devil's Hill—our folks would've had a stroke if they knew. We were the only ones with the guts to go to that weird house on Halloween. We called everything 'Our Adventures.' Remember when we beat all the fifth grade boys in the swimming races? Boy, we wouldn't let them live that down all year." She grinned. "We were *awful!* We were terrific."

"We couldn't stay children forever," I said.

"You were going to be Joan of Arc—or at least Mother Teresa. I was going to turn into this strong, together woman, tough in a good way, you know, proud, with attitude . . ." Her voice trailed off.

"All of that's still inside us. It doesn't go away." I didn't know if I truly believed that. It was something to say.

"Sometimes I feel like little pieces of me are falling off." She half smiled. "Chunks of Patty Lansing are littering Ron Gilbert's house."

I didn't want to get into one of our soul-baring conversations. Not now. It was all I could do to chew my food and swallow.

"You shouldn't have quit the swim team, L.J. You were good."

"I told you, it took up too much time." Time away from Scott. I quit right after we made up, after that terrible black-hole breakup. When I realized how restless he was.

"It's never easy," she said. "Ron, Scott. It's never easy."

I saw her through blurry eyes. Why did she keep trying to put them on the same level? Ron did such a number on her that she got to hating herself in fitting-room mirrors. Scott and I were altogether different. We were. In spite of Cara.

"What's the story with Dan Gregory?" I said. "What did he have to do with anything?"

"Well, the taping. He has a big mouth."

"What taping?"

"You didn't hear about it?"

"No."

She looked uncomfortable.

"Pat, tell me. Go ahead and spit it out."

"You know Gregory and his precious camcorder . . . They wanted to bring her back the next day and videotape it. They asked Gregory to do it, and he went straight to Gilmartin."

I closed my eyes. Dark under my eyelids, but the image kept coming through. The smell of oregano and garlic.

"L.J.—that really proves they didn't force her . . . I mean, if they thought she'd come back . . . God, can you imagine wanting it with a *mop handle*? That girl has to be something else!"

The *blip-blip-blip* of the video games echoed in my head. I couldn't brush the image away.

Mrs. Delaney and Ginny were at an away track meet that afternoon. Mr. Delaney was at work. Tommy was fooling around with the electric trains in the basement, so Scott and I had the kitchen to ourselves.

Scott was all smiles, hyper with relief. The way he swung open the refrigerator made all of Mrs. Delaney's notes on the door flutter.

"—so it's finished," he was saying. "*Finito!* The end! Her mother's not pressing charges! Want a Seven-Up? My mom went crazy and got rid of all the beer last night; I'm not supposed to drink beer anymore—what's that supposed to prove?"

"But what about the investigation?"

"Bullshit investigation." Scott laughed. "Schroeder and what's-his-name won't do anything. Schroeder came over here last night and that's it for 'investigation.' "

He shook the can of soda and pointed it at me. He was bouncing around like a three-year-old.

"Cut it out," I said. "I mean it." I was in no mood to wrestle him for it.

"OK, OK, you're no fun anymore." He

opened it over the sink and let the spray run down the drain.

"You think it's really finished?"

"Yeah, sure. They're not gonna screw over Masci's son . . . Hey, my dad didn't even ground me. Oh, he was yelling and cursing up a storm—my brains are in my dick, how could I get caught in a dumb-ass thing like that, I could have messed up with Dartmouth. I said he didn't need to tell me, I'd been beating myself up over it. It was the dumbest move I ever made. He says, OK, you make mistakes when you're a kid and you live and learn. He said he wasn't coming down hard because he knew I'd be keeping my nose clean from now on."

I took the soda from him. "What about your mom?"

"There's no way my mom's going to talk about something like that. I'm embarrassed as hell that she had to hear about it. You and Ginny, too." He was rifling through the cabinets, opening and slamming doors. "Anyway, it's over; forget about it."

"But—"

"That's all we've been talking about—drop it, OK? I found something you like, L.J."

"What?"

"Something you like. Close your eyes and open your mouth."

Sometimes the Delaneys had Hershey Kisses. I felt Scott's fingers on my lips . . . I bit down—on *raisins*! I spit them out and rushed to the sink, sputtering. I heard Scott's maniacal laugh behind me. I was gagging.

"Jesus Christ, Scott!"

"Got you!" he said.

"Moron! Asshole!" I exploded.

"What? What's the matter with you?"

"Don't you ever—don't you *ever* stick anything in my mouth! You frigging bastard! You have no right! Don't you *ever*—! Not with me!"

"*What* did you call me?"

"You frigging asshole!" I rinsed my mouth out with water from the faucet. I was shaking.

"Wash your mouth out with soap while you're at it," he said. "Can't even take a joke, can you?"

"Ha, ha. I'm going home!"

"It was only *raisins*, for crying out loud. What is that, a federal offense?"

"You *know* I hate— Just leave me alone!"

"So I was kidding around. Listen, I just got a ten-ton burden off my back. Can't you lighten up? Jeeze, I don't believe this—what got into you?"

"Raisins! Raisins got into me!"

He laughed. "I'm not gonna fight with you because it's too ridiculous. I'm not gonna fight."

I shrugged.

"This is crazy," he said. "Stop and think about it for a minute."

I was shocked by myself. I was way out of line.

"We've been under a lot of pressure. Both of us," he said.

I nodded.

"Come on, Elly, let's go up to my room and make up."

I could hear the trains running the track in the basement. Tommy spends more time playing with those trains. That's what he should have been doing that afternoon . . . instead of—

Scott trailed his finger along my arm. "Come on, we've got the place to ourselves."

Tommy knew about us; he knew not to bother us when the door to Scott's room was closed. I was always looking for a chance to be alone with Scott. Well, here we were.

He trailed his finger across my breasts. My shoulders were stiff.

"Come on, relax, babe." He smiled at me, that crooked grin I loved.

In the doorway to his room, Scott kissed me.

This was the answer to my prayers, I thought: nothing more to worry about, everything back to the way it always had been. I leaned into the warmth of his body and I tried kissing him back.

He closed the door and tipped me down on the bed. He did all the things he does, the familiar things that always made my body jump-start. My thighs stayed pressed together and he had to almost pry them apart. Scott made love to me all by himself. I wouldn't move a muscle. I didn't come. I didn't pretend.

Afterwards, Scott looked at me, but he didn't say anything.

CARA

Mommy is talking on the telephone in the kitchen. I can hear her all the way upstairs in my room through the air register. I used to hear her and that man Jim talking in the living room when he used to come over all the time. He doesn't come anymore.

She's talking to Daddy in her mean voice. It's her fault he went away.

". . . because I can't send her back to that place now . . . They gave me a song-and-dance about not setting a precedent. They provide tutoring in case of physical disability. Jesus Christ! If both her legs were broken . . . Well, look, either you help me out with a private tutor, because there's no way I can do it alone, or . . . Don't talk to me about supervision! Where've *you* been . . . ? There's less than a month left; she could finish the term in the Tenafly system and . . . I can't let her lose credit for the year."

Daddy lives in Tenafly, New Jersey. I love Daddy and my baby brother, too—he's so cute. Daddy lets me play when I'm there. He doesn't make me go over and over things, like the multiplication tables.

". . . oh, of course, by all means, discuss it with Jennifer. Let's not inconvenience Jennifer . . . All right . . . All right . . . I'm not thinking about next year, I'm thinking about right now."

Jennifer doesn't like me. I'd like her because she's pretty, but she won't let me baby-sit my little brother. She won't even let me wash her good dishes. They're so good they can't go in the dishwasher. She thinks I'll drop them. I can be careful. I don't break things.

"She seems to be handling it . . . Of course I've talked to her! Look, I couldn't follow her around . . . I can't be everywhere. OK, see if *you* can do better. Tenafly might be the answer. A different school, different surroundings . . ."

When I come down for lunch, Mommy gives me a sliced egg sandwich the way I like it, with lots of mayonnaise on toast and no lettuce.

"Am I going to Daddy's?" I say.

Mommy looks startled. "I—Cara—I don't know yet."

"Forever?"

"No, of course not! Maybe just until the end of the term. I don't know. We haven't decided."

A slice of egg drops out from between the bread. I leave it on the plate. Mommy doesn't like me to eat with my fingers.

"I don't want to go to school," I say.

"You're going to have a high school diploma! You can do it, honey. You've been doing so well."

"I don't care."

"Do you want some milk?"

"No."

"Anything to drink?"

"No."

Mommy takes her coffee and sits at the table opposite me.

"Cara—you like being at your father's, don't you?"

"Uh-huh."

I'll show Jennifer how neat I am. I'll fold all my T-shirts and underwear. I'll keep them in straight piles.

"He's coming over tonight," Mommy says.

"He is?" I jump up and clap my hands.

"When? When is he coming? Is he coming to get me?"

Daddy comes during *Wheel of Fortune*. Mommy opens the door and lets him into the living room instead of making him wait for me outside and honking the car horn. Maybe he's going to help me pack and carry the suitcase.

"Daddy!" I run to him, and he sweeps me into a bear hug. I snuggle against his chest.

He brushes the hair back from my forehead. He's so glad to see me, there are tears in his eyes. He strokes my cheek.

"Are you all right, baby?"

I nod and snuggle against him some more. His body feels so nice and warm.

"God, I wish I'd been here. When I think—," he says.

"Well, you weren't," Mommy says.

"I could kill those—"

He's wearing his navy polo shirt. I burrow in and make wrinkles in the material. I rub my face against it. I hold my arms around him tight. I want to hug, hug, hug him forever.

"OK, now," he says. He moves away from me and strokes my face. "Are you feeling OK, sweetheart?"

"*Mmmm-hmmm,*" I say.

He glances at the television set. Vanna White is wearing a sparkly blue dress.

"You can go ahead and finish your program, sweetheart," he says. "Your mother and I have to talk."

I want to be with my daddy, but I do what he says. I sit down in front of the TV. He and Mommy haven't seen each other in person for a long time. I used to think if they did, they'd make up. But they're not going to, because now he has Jennifer.

After *Who's the Boss?* they come back into the room.

"Should I go upstairs and pack?"

"No," Mommy says.

"Cara, I'm getting you a private tutor," Daddy says. "A special tutor. He'll come here, right here to the house, so you won't have to go back there anymore."

The air conditioner is on too high. I shiver.

"Am I going with you now, Daddy?"

"Well, you'll come for a visit soon, all right? Not this time but soon . . . I love you, sweetheart."

He doesn't want me.

Before he leaves, he kisses me on the cheek

and I throw my arms around him. My body gets warm against his. I feel the muscles in his back. He smells like tobacco and grass and after-shave. I close my eyes and press into him and hold him tight. It feels so good. I love my daddy. I rub against him. I rub hard.

"Cara," Mommy says.

He loosens my hands and makes me stop hugging.

"For God's sake, talk to her, Ellen." His voice is hoarse.

I want to suck my thumb, but I don't.

I get into bed and turn off the lamp on the night table. I lie in the dark. I'm not sleepy. I don't want to be all by myself with a special tutor.

Mommy comes in to say good night. She sits down on the edge of my bed.

"Can I still be in track?" I say.

"The season's almost over anyway, honey. There's only one meet left."

"Can I run in the meet?"

"I'll see. I'll talk to Mrs. Jensen."

"Mommy—am I still in the high school?"

"You'll get your credits through Shorehaven. You'll have to go in for tests. The end-of-year finals."

The bed creaks as she shifts.

"Cara—when you're in the school—I want you to stay away from those boys."

"All right." They're not my friends.

"No one's supposed to touch you. If someone wants you to do something, you say no and stay away. Remember when we talked about that?"

"You mean about sex and my private property?"

"That's right." I can't see her face in the dark.

"Not those boys," I say, "but what if *I* want to?"

"No! You can't, that's all!"

I shouldn't have asked her that. It made her mad.

I hear her take a breath and then she says, "You've got to control those feelings. You're too . . . young, honey, you're not ready for— You have to listen to me, Cara, and do as—"

"I want to go to sleep."

"Honey, it's important that you—"

"Go away!"

"Cara, that's something we have to talk about." She stands up. "All right, tomorrow."

"Close the door."

"Good night, pussycat."

"Don't call me baby names!"

My door closes on the beam of light from the hallway.

I lie on my back in the dark. It's my own private property; Mommy can't tell me! She fooled around with that man Jim. Mommy-Jim. Daddy-Jennifer. Mommy-Daddy. Everybody does. Kids on MTV. Laura Jean Kettering and Scott. Being slow in school doesn't mean I can't. It's not fair.

I draw up my knees and touch my special place. I rub it in little circles. I think about that time in the woods with Bob Dietrich. My fingers get wet and sticky. It's not so good all by myself.

Sometimes I see a boy at the gas pump when I walk by the Mobil station. He's cute. He wears cut-off jeans and a tank top. He looks at me when I walk by. I bet he wants to hug and stuff. Next time, I'll stop and hang out.

Mommy can't tell me everything.

JOE LOPEZ

I WAS WALKING DOWN THE HALL. DAN GREGORY'S back was to me; he had his locker half open. Gilhooley and DeMeo were coming the other way. It happened fast, in split seconds. Gilhooley smashed his shoulder into Gregory's back and sent his face flying into the edge of the door. The clank of metal against metal. Gregory's head rebounded and DeMeo came up behind him, gave him a hard shove back against the wall of lockers.

"Fink!"

Blood spurted from over his eye.

"Hey, cut it out!" Jesus Christ! They might have taken his eye out!

Gregory was doubled over, his hand over his face, blood seeping between his fingers. Gilhooley was crouched, ready to ram him again.

"Leave him alone," I said.

"He's the fink bastard."

"Yeah, I know, but come on, it's enough."

They'd do what I said. Gilhooley and DeMeo were freshmen, good on offense, too good for Junior V. In a couple of years, they'd be us. But for now, they looked up to me.

"If he snitched on *me*, he'd be dead, man," DeMeo said.

"It's over," I said. "It's done with. Let it go."

They shrugged and went on their way.

"Are you OK?" I said.

Dan Gregory straightened up slowly. He wiped his face and left smears of blood over a bunch of old bruises. He gave me a look of pure hate.

"Big hero," he mumbled.

Sarcastic mother. The hell with him. I left him there, leaning against the lockers, wiping his face.

So what did I expect—thank you? In his eyes, I was one of them. Well, I was, sort of. Look, you don't find a new crowd to hang with for the last three weeks of school. I could think my own thoughts and then I'd be outa here. The whole thing had blown over, anyway. Oh, there were still Cara jokes going around the school, but it was over.

Even Laura Jean Kettering was acting almost

normal with Scott again. At the beginning of the week, she was dead quiet and you could see Scott turning himself inside out, jumping all over himself to please her. The other girls were fawning over the guys, making points for sympathy. Not L.J.; you could almost hear her thinking. She always struck me as the most straight-ahead in the group.

Earlier in the week, after school on Tuesday, I'd been alone on the front steps and L.J. had come over to me.

"Hi, Joe."

"Hi."

"How's it going?"

"Pretty good."

"Got your reservations in for the Fling?"

"Yeah. I guess everybody has by now."

She was just making conversation. I could tell there was something on her mind.

"Decided who you're taking?"

"Carmen Rosado. You don't know her."

"No, I don't think so."

"She goes to Immaculate Conception."

"Oh. Well, I guess I'll meet her at the Fling. Have you been seeing her or—?"

"Sort of. On and off."

"Oh. *Uh*, Joe—there's something I've been wanting to ask you."

"Yeah, sure. Shoot."

"About that day with Cara."

I tensed up. What did she want? I wasn't sure how much she knew about Scott. "What about it?"

"I heard you'd be a friendly witness because—"

"Hey, I don't have to be a witness, for or against anybody. No one's going to court."

"—because you'd left before . . ." She let the sentence trail off. Her eyes were level with mine. "What I want to know is, what made you leave?"

"What made me leave?" I echoed.

"The others stayed and—you left. Why?"

I hesitated. "It wasn't my scene."

She kept on looking at me.

"I guess the girl was into kinky stuff and the guys got carried away with it. I didn't, that's all."

Her face was pinched. I didn't know what to say to her.

"L.J., there's no point. Don't make yourself crazy."

"I know," she'd said. "You're right."

I felt for her, and I watched her with Scott after that. She was trying—not quite holding hands with him all the time, the way they used to, but she was still definitely with him. I had this crazy thought—like, maybe if they broke up, I'd—no, that *was* crazy. I figured she needed a little time and she'd stop thinking about it. Everyone was getting back to normal, except for Dan Gregory, I guess; people were still getting their licks in. But the subject of conversation had pretty much shifted to graduation and party plans.

It was good that I didn't see Cara around school that week. I didn't want flashbacks of her standing naked, shoulders hunched and shivering, in the middle of the circle. If Dietrich hadn't made that crack at me . . . There was that moment, all of us together . . . I think I would have left anyway. I'll never know for sure.

The mop handle, though—I *told* Masci that was sick. And the videotape—I *told* him not to. That's all I could do. What else could I do?

Dan Gregory put a stop to it by blowing the whistle. Poor jerk, he was taking all that punishment for nothing because she wound up blabbing to Mrs. Jensen anyway. So now he was bleeding from a gash over his eye. For nothing.

I wondered what made him stick his neck out that way.

I wished he didn't think I was one of them.

I was the first one home that night, so I took the meat loaf out of the refrigerator and put it in the oven to heat. Meat loaf and what? I looked in the cabinet and saw the cans of beans. The hell with that—I was sick of beans. Maybe I'd wait for Mama to get in from work and she'd make something else. I know she comes home worn out but, Jeeze, I'm no cook! Where's Gloria and Dolores, anyway—they should be doing this stuff. Mercedes, too, I thought. Sixth grade is old enough.

I heard the key in the door and then Mercedes came clattering in. "What're we having?"

"Meat loaf."

She wrinkled her nose. "What else?"

"Well, what else are you making?" I said to her.

She grinned. "Me? Nothing."

"You could learn how, it's time—"

"I don't care. Susan had Twinkies at rehearsal, so I'm not hungry anyway."

"Spoiled brat," I said.

She smiled at me. "I'm not supposed to light the oven. Mama said."

She was a brat, for sure, but I couldn't help smiling back. She had a big part in the elementary school play. None of the rest of us ever got into the school things the way she did. She was going to be something.

I took out a can. "OK, so we'll have beans again."

She started hopping around in one of her little dances and sang, "Beans, beans, black and strong, make you fart all night long."

She made me laugh.

I used the can opener and she settled down at the kitchen table, watching me.

"Joe, what's a blow job?"

I almost dropped the damn can. "What?"

"I don't know what it means."

Jesus Christ!

"The kids at rehearsal said a girl at the high school got gang banged because she was giving out blow jobs. Ellen's sister told her and— What's gang banged? Is it sex?"

I didn't know what to do; I exploded. "I oughta wash your mouth out with soap!"

"I'm just asking . . ."

I was close to slapping her. "Shut up!"

I saw the hurt look on her face turning stony. What was I yelling at her for? Mother of God, she was only a little kid.

"Mercedes," I said. "You're supposed to talk to Mama about—no, not Mama—ask Gloria or Dolores."

She shrugged. I knew she wouldn't. I knew she wouldn't ask me anything again, either. I didn't know how to talk to her. Jesus Christ!

"Where did you hear that?"

She was staring at the tabletop.

"Mercedes. Where?"

"I *told* you, at rehearsal. Not just at rehearsal. All the kids in school are saying things."

How in hell did it get to the elementary school and into my sister's mouth? I could picture all of these little kids coming home to their parents . . . It was going to spread all over the damn town!

LAURA JEAN

IT HAD BEEN A LONG DAY—SCHOOL AND THEN
Foodtown—and my head was still beeping from
the cash register. All I wanted was to relax for
a minute, but Mom flew at me as soon as I opened
the kitchen door. She didn't even give me a
chance to put my things down.

"I heard something today that was— I was at
the Women's League meeting and Anita Dailey
was talking about— I'm so shocked, I— They
kept saying 'your daughter's boyfriend.' "

I felt the muscles in the back of my neck
tightening. "What?"

"About that rape. About Bob Dietrich and
the Delaney boys and—"

My stomach cramped. "It wasn't rape! It's not
what you think."

"Even the youngest children are coming home
with questions. Anita Dailey's Maureen . . .
How do you explain that to a little girl?" She

winced and closed her eyes. "A bottle and a mop."

"It wasn't like that! They don't know what they're talking about. It wasn't a regular bottle and Scott wasn't the one who—"

"So you know all about it and I'm the last to hear? I didn't know what to say to them. Right now—honestly, I don't know what to say to you."

I didn't know what to say to her, either.

The refrigerator hummed between us. The copper pans on the rack were catching the last glint of sunlight.

"Mom, you know Scott. You know he wouldn't—"

"Your crowd, Laura Jean. They said Bob Dietrich and John Masci and the Delaney brothers."

"That girl was after him; you *know* he wouldn't—"

I saw the confusion and pain in Mom's face. I felt tears welling up in my eyes. I was going to reach for her hand, but then she said, "All I could think of to say was that you're not seeing Scott anymore."

"How could you! How could you say that!" Mom was crazy about Scott, he was over here all the time, I mean, she used to make that sour-cream cake especially for him.

"I didn't want to believe— I couldn't believe what I was hearing. I sat there, I was numb. I never would have expected something like that, but— I don't want you mixed up in—"

"There was a whole bunch of guys. It wasn't Scott's fault."

"Whatever. It doesn't matter. Just keep away from him."

"I can't believe you!" I exploded. "I can't believe you'd turn on him like that! Without even knowing the whole—"

Her voice became shrill. "He's not my child, Laura Jean, and you are. You have to stop dating him."

Dating? What was she talking about? We weren't *dating*; I loved him! The kitchen passage was narrow and I was backed up against the sink. The edge of the counter cut into my hips.

She kept talking and talking at me.

"I never imagined . . . Boys from nice homes, from Shorehaven! Drugs and who knows what . . ."

"Scott doesn't do drugs! What are you talking about? That's crazy! Did you ever see him on drugs? Did you?"

"I don't understand. I don't know what you've been doing."

"You think we've been sitting around smoking crack?" I stuck out my arm; it was shaking. "You want to check for needle marks?"

She grabbed my arm, not looking at it, pressing her fingertips into my flesh. "I have to ask you—" She had the strangest look on her face, embarrassment and panic. "Laura Jean—" I knew I didn't want to hear what she was going to ask.

"I have to know—have you— Laura Jean, has he ever done sick things with you?"

"No!" I screamed. "No! What's wrong with you? He's still *Scott*. He doesn't do drugs. Nothing. He never did anything!"

She wasn't listening to anything I said. "I don't want you with that crowd anymore, do you hear me?"

Her face was inches from mine.

The pulse in the back of my neck pounded. I brushed by her, brushed past the refrigerator.

"I have your reputation to worry about and—"

I ran up the stairs and her voice followed me.

"Where are you going? Listen to me, I—"

"You don't know anything!" I yelled.

I slammed the door of my room and sat down on the bed. I thought I was going to be sick to my stomach. It was so unfair! Mom's friends knew he was my boyfriend because she was always bragging about him—I'd hear her on the phone. Like getting Scott was my major accomplishment; that annoyed the hell out of me, but still. And now—talk about peer pressure!

I lost my respect for Mom right then and there. You don't trash someone the minute there's trouble. She didn't know me at all if she thought I'd desert Scott now, no matter what anyone said.

Mom didn't once ask how I was feeling.

"Drugs and who knows what." He doesn't even smoke! He cares so much about keeping in shape. He's always scrubbed and clean. My stomach turned over. I loved the way he looked when he came up from the lockers after a shower, his hair curled up damp on the back of his neck. And they were talking about him. Crucifying him!

I'd been giving him a hard time, that was the truth. Punishing him, all because my pride was hurt. OK, I wish he'd walked—why didn't he just leave, like Joe Lopez—but he was on the spot. In front of all the guys, that girl asked him to screw her. Boys can be such babies about proving their manhood. That's all he did, that didn't make him a doper or some kind of pervert!

The thought of Anita Dailey and everyone repeating those awful lies made me double over.

We were supposed to be looking forward to a good time, the time of our lives. It was supposed to be *over* and we were being sucked back into a nightmare.

JOE LOPEZ

Tony Edison is Shorehaven's own celebrity.
I saw him all the time on the five o'clock or
eleven o'clock news. The first time I saw him in
person, he was emceeing at a donkey basketball
game in the gym for the benefit of the new science wing. The thought that came into my mind
was: *He looks just like himself.* I'd never say something that dumb out loud, but, wouldn't you
know, Mike Clay did.

"Hey, he looks just like himself," Clay said.

"Moron," I said. "Who the hell did you think
he'd look like?"

Tony Edison's kids go to the Ocean Point
elementary school and he was always lending his
name to something. So when I saw him in the
parking lot when I came to school that morning,
I figured it was for another fund-raiser.

He was with a woman carrying a clipboard
and a guy with one of those hand-held cameras,

and there were a lot of kids standing around them.

I saw Verna Baker on the fringe. "What's happening?" I asked her.

Verna brushed the hair away from her eyes. She's got bangs that cover her eyes like a screen and she's always fiddling with them, pushing them back. It could make you crazy.

"He's asking questions," she said. "About that girl. Cara."

"*What?*"

Holy shit! I stood back and watched. Some asshole was talking to him a mile a minute. And when John Masci came walking by, the asshole pointed at him.

"John Masci?" Edison called.

Masci stopped. "That's me," he said, with a grin.

You watch something starting and there's not a damn thing you can do to stop it. I stood there, paralyzed, thinking, Masci, you dumb cluck, keep moving, you don't know . . .

"Mayor Masci's son, right?" Edison was holding a mike.

"Right, that's me."

The guy with the camera was moving into his face and Masci was oblivious, grinning.

"In Shorehaven, Long Island, the police are 'investigating' the alleged brutal gang rape of a retarded girl by a group of high school athletes, one of whom happens to be the son of the town's mayor."

Masci's grin had faded and his face collapsed. His eyes darted back and forth helplessly. Then he turned tail, ran toward the steps, and the camera kept pointing at his back.

"The police chief here is appointed by the mayor, and the 'investigation' has dragged on with a singularly curious lack of energy. This affluent suburb's silence . . ."

I tried edging away, nonchalantly, fighting the sudden shakiness in my legs. If that S.O.B. stuck a camera in my face, I'd ram it down his throat.

I saw Scott and Laura Jean coming up the back path toward the parking lot. L.J. was walking a little ahead of him, shaking her head about something. Then Goren was there, talking to them, and their faces turned grim.

They walked quickly along the edge of the lot, Laura Jean clutching Scott's arm. They had made it to the bottom of the front stairs when, with a burst of movement, Edison and his crew caught up to them.

"Are you Scott Delaney?"

"No." Scott's lips twisted in some semblance of a smile. "I'm Goldberg. Sam Goldberg."

Laura Jean was wide-eyed and pale. She was hanging on to Scott's arm in a death grip.

They turned and continued up the stairs, the cameraman following their backs. They were almost at the front door when the woman with the clipboard got her bright idea.

"Hey, Scott!" she called.

He automatically turned around. Then, realizing he'd been had, he flushed and told her what she could do to herself.

That night, it was on the five o'clock news and the eleven o'clock news. It was repeated on the network news at five-thirty and eleven-thirty. Tony Edison on the local station, Brad Carver for the network. Shots of John Masci, flustered and running. Yearbook photos of Dietrich, Clay, and both Delaneys. The outside of the Delaneys' house, the azaleas in the front blooming bright orange. "A retarded girl . . . a bottle and mop handle . . . affluent Long Island community . . . cover-up . . . high school leaders, football star, hockey captain . . ."

By the next night, the other channels had picked up the story; over and over, clips of the President, the wreckage of a plane in Texas, and

Scott Delaney—audio bleeped out, but you could tell the words he was mouthing coast-to-coast, while a white-faced Laura Jean clutched his arm.

Every time I saw it, the shakiness in my legs kicked in again.

LAURA JEAN

THEY WERE EVERYWHERE. MR. GILMARTIN KEPT them off school property, but they crowded at the gates. They waited in front of the Delaneys' house. They were everywhere, shoving each other, calling out to Scott or Bob or John or Clay, trying to goad them into saying something, anything.

On TV they caught Mrs. Delaney coming out of her house. "How do you feel about your sons'—?" They showed Mrs. Delaney stunned, biting her lip, before she ran back inside.

They printed the yearbook pictures. Scott's cocky grin under the "Jocks Abuse Retarded Girl" headline. Bob smiling past "The Cover-up Town."

Nothing was private anymore. We were being picked over, picked clean, by a frenzy of feeding sharks. They uncovered that Halloween years ago when Scott and Mike Clay broke the library window. They printed a quote from a teacher: "Those boys were given a sense of entitlement . . ." And about Bob: "Star football player, the adopted son of the CEO of—" I'd never known Bob was adopted; I didn't think anyone did.

The phone rang at our house. Dad called, "It's for you," and I picked it up. The woman's voice said, "L.J.?"—*L.J.*—and for a second, I thought it was my sister Anne. Then, "You're Scott Delaney's girlfriend, aren't you? What's your reaction to—?" I dropped the receiver, quick. We kept it off the hook for the rest of that evening.

Scott was lying low. He stayed home from school the next day, and I could picture him cornered in his room, stir crazy and hounded. I tried calling him and got nothing but busy signals.

After school, I asked Mom to drive me to the Delaneys'.

"No," she said. "No, don't get involved."

"I *am* involved," I said. "So will you drive me or not? Look, they're camped in front of his house—I can't walk past."

"I won't let you go there! Seeing you on TV was— Daddy and I talked last night and—"

"You won't *let* me?" I was furious. "Are you

planning to physically stop me?" I needed to be with him. I needed to be with him right then.

I punched out Pat's number on the phone. I couldn't stop pacing while I waited for her to come. Finally, I heard her driving around to the backyard and I ran out. Mom's voice drifted behind me. "Don't go! Laura Jean! Listen—"

I jumped into the car and crouched low in the front seat.

"It's OK," Pat said. "No one's in front of your house."

I held my crouch. "You never know, they might—"

"You're getting paranoid." She drove along Sycamore. "I swear to God, there's no one on the street. A squirrel, that's it." I felt the car swerve as she made the left onto Oak. Eight blocks and another left onto Dogwood.

"*Uh-oh,*" she said.

"What?"

"There's a mob in front of Scott's."

I curled myself below the seat. "Drive to the back. Floor it!"

"They're blocking the driveway, L.J."

"Just go! Run them down!"

"Yeah, sure."

I felt her creeping along, honking and

honking the horn. I heard their voices coming at us. I kept my head down. There was a mildew spot in the carpeting. My legs were cramped.

"All right, we're in the backyard," Pat said. "What now?"

"Get me next to the garage."

"This is so weird. Like playing cops and robbers."

"Right alongside the garage door."

"OK, you've got it."

"Thanks. Thanks a million."

Pat kind of laughed. "Sure, anytime."

I sprinted out of the car and to the garage door. Please, let it be unlocked. They'd always kept it unlocked, but now—

I pulled the handle and it swung upward. I pushed it down behind me. In the dim light, I picked my way toward the hall door through dark shapes. A jumble of things. Two old sleds protruded from wall hooks. A rake and shovels. Outgrown hockey sticks leaned against a barrel, one of them broken. Scott had kept the broken handle because Bobby Nystrom's autograph was on it. That was from years ago, when he'd skated at Cantiague where the Islanders practiced and Nystrom had come onto the ice and given him tips. I remembered him showing it to me, his

eyes lighting up, reliving the little-kid thrill.
Paint cans in a pyramid. A metal saucer against
the wall. We'd taken it up to the hill last winter
and flown through the snow. We'd laughed and
laughed, and my jeans got soaked through. A
basketball. The rusted remains of a child-size
bike. Artifacts of a regular kid growing up. Why
were they doing this to him?

My knock on the metal door to the hall made
it rattle. Mrs. Delaney's "Who is it?" was cau-
tious and frightened.

"Laura Jean. It's Laura Jean." My breath came
fast, like sobs.

Scott was alone in his room. The shade was
down. He needed a shave.

"Jeeze, I'm glad you came!" He grabbed me
in a bear hug. We held on to each other, tight.
And then the hug turned into a need that made
us both pant. We kissed, a deep bruising kiss,
tasting each other. Scott couldn't let go of me;
he moved me over to the door with him while
he locked it.

"Your mother—," I said.

"No one'll come in."

We grabbed for each other, urgently, blindly, no time to take our clothes off. My pants

remained in a tangle below my knees. His zipper scraped against my stomach. Nothing could have pried us apart. We were frantic, maybe even more than at the very beginning. We hadn't been like that for a long time.

Afterwards, we rested, spent, on his bed.

"I'm glad you're here," he said.

His mother in the house. Reporters outside! "We took a big chance," I said.

His arm was around my shoulders. "God, I needed you," he said.

I studied the faint cracks on the ceiling. I thought, it was like this when my grandma Margaret died last year. I really loved her and it was the first time someone close to me had died. The whole world turned gray; there was the taste of ashes in my mouth. I thought my sadness would never end, but in the middle of mourning her, I kept wanting sex. The day before the funeral and two days after, I got Scott to make love to me. I felt ashamed for wanting it at a time like that, but I couldn't help it. I felt like a monster for a long time. Then I read somewhere that when there's a death, the life force comes up strong. Sex bubbles up to remind you that you're alive.

"I'm not coming back to school," Scott said.

I looked at his drawn face. "What do you mean?"

"Gilmartin called the house last night. He wants all of us to stay home from school—too disruptive with the press crowding around us. They're giving us tutors."

"Oh, Scott."

"That part's all right. Only a couple of weeks left."

"It's not fair!"

"Nobody gives a shit about fair. We can't go to graduation, either. None of us. We'll get our diplomas in the mail. Because those bastards would ruin it for everybody."

I could see that. Graduation was always at the field; there'd be no way to keep the reporters away.

"Gilmartin's worrying about everything except my rights. I've got a right to be at my own graduation, damn it! The hell with it, who cares about parading around in some stupid gown. It's all Mickey Mouse, anyway."

How much he cared was all over his face.

"Laura Jean?"

"What?"

"The same with the Fling."

I couldn't talk. I turned my face into the pillow.

"Those bastards! I'm sorry. I know you went out and bought a new dress and . . . Damn it!" He punched his fist into his hand. "Maybe you could . . . Can you return it?"

I shook my head.

"I'm sorry," he said. "Jeeze, I wish—" He repeated, "I wish . . ." and then let his voice trail off.

The beautiful emerald green dress, hanging in my closet. I'd taken all the tags off. I was having shoes dyed to match at Brustein's.

"Those friggin' bastards! The newspapers are hanging us!"

Well, there'd be dances at Dartmouth, I thought, and . . . Dartmouth?

"Charlie Goren's going. Listen, he'd take you along with Marie—"

I shook my head. "I don't want to be with anyone else."

He moved his head restlessly against the pillow. "We're going to get screwed over, L.J."

"It can't be in the papers forever."

"The Shorehaven police are off the case. Nassau County's taking over. They're talking about a grand jury—"

"Grand jury?"

"To decide if we get indicted."

"Indicted?"

"A trial. Rape and assault. I have to get a lawyer. My dad's talking to—"

"No!" I said. "No! That can't happen! You didn't—"

"It'll happen." His words were chopped and bitter. "They're out for blood. No one cares about the truth. Nassau County's gonna be so worried about them screaming cover-up, they'll nail us, no matter what."

"But Cara's lying!"

We lay side by side for a long time, silent, staring up at the ceiling.

"I hear them in my head all the time, yelling questions at me," he said. I felt his arm contract. "Even when they're not here. I keep hearing them in my head."

He pulled me close and rubbed his mouth roughly against mine. His kiss made my teeth cut into my lips. We made love again, and I knew it was to hold down the fear.

CARA

Scott and Bob and all of them are on TV and in the newspapers. Bob's yearbook picture is on the front page, the one I like so much, where he's smiling and so handsome.

They talk about me on the TV and in the newspapers. They call me the retarded girl. Why are they calling me bad names? In the *Post*, it says my I.Q. is 70.

I ask Mommy, "Is seventy bad?"

"No, honey," she says. "It's not bad."

They write about me fooling around with the boys. Not my name, but everyone knows it's me. Daddy and Jennifer and Anne Pierce and Valerie and everybody knows all my personal things. Nothing is personal property anymore when everybody knows.

"Mommy, I want to go away," I say. "Can we go away?"

I went to the drugstore with Mommy yesterday

and an old lady said, "She's the one." People were looking at me.

"Does the *New York Times* go outside of New York?" I ask Mommy.

She says yes.

TV is coast-to-coast. That means from here to California. I know Texas is next to California. I'm not retarded.

I want to go far away.

I stay home all the time.

I lost all my friends.

LAURA JEAN

YOU'D THINK NOTHING WAS HAPPENING ANY-where else in the world. The newspapers kept running the story; I don't know which one started the "Cover-up Town" thing, but they all picked it up and so Shorehaven became the sub-urb from hell. Cover-up Town—it had a phony ring to it, like the title of a trashy novel.

Dad always used to bring the *New York Post* home—he'd read it on the train—and I'd look at Ann Landers and the horoscopes. On Sun-days, we'd get the *New York Times*; it had the best fashion ads and sometimes I'd read the mag-azine section. I guess I mostly got news from TV. Now I bought all the papers, first thing, every single day; I couldn't help it, even though it felt like I was twisting the knife.

The *New York Post* kept us in the headlines. "Jock Jekyll and Hydes." The *New York Times* moved it off the front page, but they had a long article inside about everybody's psychology. The reporter never even *met* the guys, but all of a sudden he was an expert on them; he used quotes from anybody that had something bad to say.

I used to assume that what I read was true, just because it was in print. I was learning how easily anything can be slanted.

What hurt most was seeing Scott's photo. On a newspaper page, in black and white and out of context, his grin seemed cocky and arrogant. He's not like that; it's because his smile is crooked that it looks that way. I remembered the day the yearbook pictures were taken. We'd been sitting in the sun on the front steps with Charlie Goren, waiting for our turns and kidding around. Scott borrowed my comb and used my sunglasses for a mirror. I wore my pink silk blouse; it didn't go with my shorts and sandals at all, but I knew they wouldn't show in the photo and it was too hot for anything else. Scott said I was dressed like a split personality. He'd innocently posed for a school photo, and the newspapers had stolen and shifted his image.

Some people made statements defending the town. Mrs. Carlin, the president of the PTA, was quoted about how great our library and our school system were, and it wasn't fair to give the whole town a black eye because of less than a dozen kids. "Why don't you interview our National Merit Scholarship finalists?" she said. "Or the Scoutmaster? We have a huge number of boys and girls involved in scouting."

Bob Dietrich and John Masci used to be Boy Scouts. Bob stayed with it for a while, and I think he almost made Eagle Scout, but then he put all his time into football practice instead. So what was that supposed to prove?

Mr. Krieski from the Stop 'n' Shop said Shorehaven was a good place, friendly and family-oriented, and incidents like that happen all over, so why single out one town? There's nothing wrong with Shorehaven, he said, except that Tony Edison happens to live here.

A lot of quotes like that were published, all defending the reputation of Shorehaven. No one defended the guys. No one. I knew the kids at school were on their side, but I guess their parents pretty well muzzled them. Beating up Dan Gregory was meant as a show of support; I think it might have taken on a life of its own.

I heard Dan stayed out for a while, but then he came back again. I heard some guys got his camcorder out of his locker and he went berserk when they smashed it. I passed him in the hall; we didn't say hello and he looked away first. His black eyes had turned yellowish. His lips were very swollen, distorted, with what looked like a fresh, raw cut. He looked bad, bad enough to make me feel terrible—but he'd been friendly with Scott for years, he lived right next door, for God's sake, and I didn't *want* to feel sorry for him. Well, he'd taken a lot of punishment and it served no purpose at all.

There had to be a way to show Scott's side of the story. "Jekyll and Hydes"! Those guys weren't monsters. Someone had to stand up for them.

The reporters weren't around in such big clusters anymore, but I could have found some. I thought about talking to them, but I was afraid I'd freeze and mess up. That day on the school steps, I'd been numb; I'd felt like an opossum caught in the glare of headlights. I've seen that clip on TV. I don't really remember any of it. I was too numb. *Talking to reporters would be altogether different from talking in real life*, I thought. I liked to watch beauty pageants on TV, I guess to compare myself to the contestants. At the personality part, when they had to answer a question, I always thought I could do a million times better. I always had terrific answers right on the tip of my tongue—I mean, I should have been a shoo-in for Miss America. Now I know that it's a lot easier in your own living room than in front of a TV camera.

I could write a letter to the papers, telling Scott's side of it. Writing gave me some control. It wouldn't help much, but it was a beginning, at least until I thought of something else.

I played Tammy Wynette's "Stand by Your Man" over and over again. It was comforting; it made me feel strong and ready for action. Mom kept screaming at me to turn it off, as though it was meant as an attack on her.

The *New York Times*, the *New York Post*, the *Long Island Press*, *Newsday*. I found the addresses of their editorial offices. I rewrote the letter in my loose-leaf until I got it right, and then I typed it on regular stationery. I knew my name turning up in print would really tear it with my parents, but I barely hesitated when I dropped the four envelopes in the mailbox.

Someone from the *Times* called me a few days later. He was checking to make sure I was the one who had written; I didn't know they did that, but I guess it's a good idea. And he told me which day it would run.

I was talking to Pat about it. "He sounded so snobby, kind of English, and he acted like he was giving me some kind of award. Like getting a letter into the *Times* was a big deal and I should grovel with gratitude."

"It is a big deal," Pat said. "That's a big deal newspaper."

"I guess."

"Something published in the *New York Times* would have been *terrific* with your college applications. Too bad it's too late."

"What?"

"It would have been so impressive, L.J."

I looked at her. "Right. Any college would be impressed with a letter defending my rapist boyfriend."

Pat put her hand over her mouth. "Oh . . . I didn't think . . ."

"Even better if he was a murderer. That would make me stand out from the crowd."

We started laughing. I hadn't laughed deep and hard in a long time. We were almost hysterical.

"Or if he was on death row—," Pat said, choking.

"Great essay. A personal opinion on capital punishment, from intimate contact with—"

"Well researched and sincere."

"And between visits to the slammer, I maintained a B average and participated in cheerleading, swimming, student government, science fair, orchestra, newspaper, candy-striping, and—" I finally caught my breath. "God, we're losing it."

"I don't know how I came out with that," Pat said. "That kind of thing makes Ron look at me like I've got two heads. I embarrass him."

"Come on, Pat. You're *funny*. You've still got a hangover from college applications, that's all."

"Maybe."

I suddenly felt terrible. "I should have said 'alleged.'"

"What?" Pat asked.

"Alleged rapist. Because he's not. I didn't mean—"

"I know that, L.J. You don't need to tell me. I know you were just clowning."

None of it was funny. Not me, not Scott, not Pat. If Ron Gilbert loved her at all, it wasn't for the real Pat that I knew. I wondered about Scott, too. That soft, sweet girl-that-I-marry girl, the girl he'd protect and would never ask to do certain things—she wasn't *me*, never had been. And I loved Scott because . . . maybe because I got hooked on him back in seventh grade by the way his hair fell. I suppose love doesn't have much to do with real, logical reasons. The point was, I *loved* him.

JOE LOPEZ

Around school I was mostly hanging with Charlie Goren. Without the others around, there wasn't much action. Too quiet, not much fun. One time I tried sitting at the Latino table in the cafeteria, with guys from when I played Latin League soccer. To tell the truth, I couldn't go back to being in that ghetto again; it's not like I was forgetting who I am, but I was used to belonging with the elite, knowing everybody, everybody knowing me.

I went to see John Masci at his house one night after dinner. We sat on his back porch in the dark. Insects kept hitting against the screening.

"Tina broke up with me," he blurted out.

"She did?"

"Yeah. She wanted to go to the Fling." It was too dark to see the look on his face. "She'll find someone else to ask her in a minute."

"Well—," I started.

"She broke up with me on the phone. One sentence, just like that. Like it didn't mean anything."

I felt bad for him. I thought all along that Tina was with him only because he was a senior and a jock. Maybe everyone knew that except for John.

"I did everything for her, everything she wanted, I mean it. I never liked any girl that much before . . ."

"Hey, forget her, there are other girls."

"Yeah, forget her." His voice broke. "I've got other things to worry about. My dad's getting a lawyer."

"Your dad's cool now?"

"I guess. Every once in a while, he looks at me and cuffs me across the head. I never know when it's coming." A strangled laugh. "Keeps me jumping."

"You're getting your own lawyer? I thought—"

"I know, I thought we were all in it together. But then Mr. Dietrich got some big lawyer just for Bob; he's gonna cut his own deal. Everyone's on their own. So then the Delaneys got someone and—all for one and one for all, just like Coach taught us, right?"

"It'll be OK," I said. I sounded lame.

"No, I'm in deep shit." He cleared his throat a couple of times. "The Dietrichs are something else. Did you know Bob was adopted?"

"I read it in the paper."

"Me, too. That was the first I heard it. You know what Mr. Dietrich said to him? 'Blood always tells.' "

"Jesus!"

We sat there, thinking about it. I watched the tree branches moving against the sky.

John's shoulders were slumped forward. "Tina and me—she thought I was funny, she laughed at everything . . . She was so pretty. Everyone liked her, right?"

"Yeah. She seemed OK."

"I took her out to good places. I called her all the time."

I thought I heard him snuffling. I hoped he wasn't crying. I didn't want to know.

"Christ almighty, I wish it hadn't happened!" he burst out. "I wish I hadn't been there! One friggin' afternoon! I wish—I wish—"

"Look, your dad's mayor and that ain't Swiss cheese. And you'll have a good lawyer."

They'd pull strings for him. He had the nice house with the grill in the backyard and the station wagon in the garage and the collie named Rover and the screened-in porch where they drank lemonade in the summertime. People like that always get protected.

John blew his nose. "It wasn't *me*, I didn't do anything . . . I watched, that's all. Anybody would, right . . . ? Since when is *looking* a crime?"

After all this, he still didn't have a clue that he'd done anything wrong. I didn't have a single thing to say to him.

LAURA JEAN

TODAY WAS THE DAY. I WANTED TO PICK UP THE *Times* first thing, but there wasn't time. It was finals week and I was late; I had to rush to school. The French test was in the morning. I was pretty sure I'd passed, but I didn't do well. I hadn't been able to concentrate on studying. Math and Holocaust studies were going to be back to back the next day. I was OK for Holocaust studies— I couldn't forget any of it, not the lady who came to speak to us that day nor all the talk about "the other"—but I needed to review the math. Anyway, I had to stop at the newsstand first.

I was going down the stairs after French when I saw her coming up, hugging the banister. Cara Snowden! I hadn't seen her since . . . I stopped short and stared. She was dressed in pale pink: pink shorts, pink top, pink socks, pink ribbon in blond hair. The Ivory girl. I was paralyzed and shaking with anger.

She saw me staring and she stopped, too, about ten steps below me. She looked up at me cautiously, holding a loose-leaf in front of her chest. She hesitated and then she half smiled and said, "Hi, Laura Jean." Her voice went up, like a question.

I raced down the stairs past her, on the far side so I wouldn't brush against her; I couldn't have handled the slightest accidental touch. I wanted to strangle her. Was she still hallucinating that I was her *friend*, after all she had done!

I was still shaking inside as I walked to the newsstand on Main Street.

I bought the *Times*. I didn't want to open it right on Main Street; it was too public. I walked another block to the railroad station and sat down on an empty bench outside the station house. A headline about the Middle East. A full-page ad for Saks Fifth Avenue. Tight columns of print that could have been hieroglyphics. Then—Letters to the Editor. I skimmed the page. Mine was near the bottom. "Laura Jean Kettering." It felt strange to see my name in print. I read the letter. My words, exactly, but there were different line breaks that made them seem unfamiliar. I was excited and terribly self-conscious all at the same time. "You're spoiling the end of senior year . . ." was stupid in print. I should have left that out and just concentrated on the injustice . . .

But *my letter* was in the *New York Times!* People everywhere would be reading it. I had done something; I had fought back for Scott!

I wondered if my folks had seen it yet. Even if they didn't get the paper, they'd hear about it. I'd deal with that later. Math or no math, I wasn't going home. I headed for the Delaneys'.

There were new lines around Mrs. Delaney's eyes. She looked drawn, but she kept up the bright smile. "Come on in. The boys are in Mineola; they're meeting with Mr. Romano."

Mr. Romano. The lawyer.

I followed her into the kitchen. "Did you see the letter?" I said.

"First thing this morning. You said just what needed to be said. It made Scott feel so much more confident and—"

"I should have left out the part about—"

"No, it was excellent. Perfect. Scott wanted to call you, but you were in school and then he had to . . . How about lunch? Tuna salad, or ham and cheese, or I have left-over meat loaf and—" She was rattling off the choices, as though she were trying to hold on to normal things, kitchen things.

"I'm not really hungry."

"I know." She nodded and sagged into the chair opposite me. "I'm not, either."

She was the only one who understood how I felt. And it had to be worse for her than anyone, with Tommy and Scott both.

"You have to eat, hon," she said. "You have to keep up your strength."

"I do. Honest."

"Maybe a little tuna—?"

I shook my head.

"OK, no more nagging."

I could see how tired she was, but no matter what, she held everything together.

"I'll make coffee for us," I said. I went to the refrigerator and took out the jar of instant. With my back to her, I said, "I've been wanting to ask you— I couldn't bring it up with Scott— What about Dartmouth? Has he heard anything?"

"No. I don't know. If he's not *indicted*—I don't see how they can withdraw an offer because of a false accusation. They can't do that!"

I put the water on the stove to boil. "What does Mr. Romano say? About—an indictment?"

"What, with this press persecution— If it happens, we'll deal with it." Her voice was steel. "It can't come to that. A grand jury has to have some sense of fairness. My boys are— It's ridiculous— After all, what did they actually do? That girl has some kinky tastes and, OK, they showed bad judgment in going along with it, but boys being boys has never been a *crime*. They'd have to lock up most of the teenage boys in this country!"

She was like a mother lion defending her cubs. "You're the strongest person I know," I said.

"No, just spitting angry! I toss and turn all night long, just furious! How dare that—that girl—ruin lives—"

I took our cups to the table and sat down. "I feel the same way. Just this morning, I—"

She nodded. "I know you do. The way you're standing by him—you're the best thing in the world for him right now."

" 'Stand by your man,' " I said.

She smiled. "This is a terrible time, but you and Scott will get past it and go on, even stronger." She sipped at her coffee and it looked like she was having a hard time swallowing. "I believe in God and the power of prayer. It will all come out right in the end."

"I hope so." I sighed. "I'd never say this to

anyone else, but— I still don't understand. Why did he—? How could he—?"

"It had nothing at all to do with how he feels about you," she said abruptly. "Nothing at all." The napkin in her hands was being pulled to tatters. "Take it from me, Laura Jean—don't think about it."

"I wish I knew how to stop. Sometimes I—"

"For God's sake! Your—your *brooding* isn't going to help anything, is it?" I was taken aback by the sharpness of her tone.

Mrs. Delaney picked up her cup and saucer and carried them to the sink. She held her shoulders straight; she had wonderful posture. I heard the gurgle as she poured the rest of her coffee down the drain.

I felt miserable. She was the only one I could talk to without feeling disloyal, but I shouldn't have said anything.

There was a silence that grew and grew. I looked at her back. I wondered if she was mad at me.

Finally, she turned around.

"Scott loves you," she said, "you love him, and you'll make an adorable couple."

She was handing him over to me, with her blessing. No more about exciting new opportunities. She had to be scared, really scared.

JOE LOPEZ

I'D HEARD THE ROGER COLLINS TALK SHOW WAS doing the whole hour about it. "Gang Rapes" or "Youth Packs" or something; I didn't get home in time for the very beginning.

I turned on the TV in the middle of Tony Edison telling how he got wind of the story when his son came home from elementary school asking questions. Just like Mercedes.

There was a psychologist talking about male bonding. He said, "When athletic teams get involved in group serial sex—they call it 'pulling train'—along with the obvious antiwoman aggression, there's a component of homoeroticism."

Say what? Jocks hate fags worse than anybody! Look at the way Tommy Delaney kept beating up on Alex Maitland.

Some woman from Shorehaven talked about what a good town it was, a regular American town, maybe a little more affluent, and she never came to any point. And people from the audience kept yelling stuff about if it was such a good town, how come everyone knew and no one did anything until Edison reported it?

"Your ratings superseded the interests of your own town," she said furiously to Edison. "It could have been handled quietly, but you had to turn it into a circus."

After the commercial, the Shorehaven woman was all red in the face and flustered; they must have been picking on her during the break.

There was a black lawyer talking about that Central Park jogger case a few years back; he kept talking about racism in the press, because the Shorehaven gang was called "jocks" and the Central Park gang was called a "wolf pack." It was exactly the same thing, he said, but only the black kids were described as animals. Someone yelled, "Right on!"

Jesus, they had it all wrong! I was on the edge of my chair—it wasn't the same. Were they crazy?

Then a lady from N.O.W. started talking about pornography and violence. "This culture constantly commercializes sex; women are presented as objects. Permission is granted to dehumanize." The discussion went way off the track. Seemed like everyone on the panel was working on getting his own pet thing in.

Collins went into the audience the way he does. He rushed down the aisles with the mike, giving different people a chance to talk. Everybody was waving their hands at him. Some man said if mothers weren't out working on account of this women's lib thing, then there'd be someone home to teach kids wrong from right. Yeah, sure. If Mama wasn't out working, we wouldn't be eating.

Everyone was looking to put blame someplace. People in the audience were saying things like "It's always jocks, because they think they're entitled . . ." One lady got mad at that: "Athletes work hard for excellence!" She said her son was an Olympic diver and proud to represent his country. I was with her. I trained hard, I lifted weights and shit, I went for my personal best, and I'm proud of it.

Collins took calls from viewers at home. I bet those calls are pre-arranged, because Laura Jean Kettering got through right away. He didn't say her name; he said the girlfriend of one of the Shorehaven boys. I knew L.J.'s voice.

She started off strong. "I've known those boys

for years and I want to tell you the truth about them. They're law-abiding. They keep in training, they go to church, almost all of them plan to go on to college. They respect women—their mothers, sisters, girlfriends. They didn't *force* that girl to do anything, they wouldn't, and anyone who knows them would back me up on that. There was no crime involved. They're not criminals," she said. "What you were saying before—it was nothing like that Central Park jogger. It wasn't the same thing at all. They're not muggers or rapists. They'd never beat up a woman. They wouldn't in a million years pull a runner off a track. If they'd been in the park that day, they would have jumped in and defended her in a minute. I *know* that."

People in the audience started yelling, "A rape is a rape!"

"You don't understand—," L.J. said.

They were shouting her down. "A rape is a rape!"

"You don't understand," she kept repeating. "You don't understand." She sounded like she was trying not to cry.

"A rape is a rape!"

She couldn't get anything else out. I felt for

her. Anyway, she was dead right. In Central Park, we would have been heroes.

Tomorrow, Collins announced, the subject would be prostitutes with children. The show ended with a soda commercial, a circle of cans surrounding bimbos in bikinis.

LAURA JEAN

THE COLLINS SHOW IS TAPED FOR LATER BROAD-
cast, so I was able to turn it on the next day and
hear myself. Dad had come home early from work
to see it. He and Mom sat beside me on the
living room couch. There was an edgy silence
between us.

I thought I did well as long as I stayed with
what I'd planned to say. I sneaked a look at Dad.
I hoped he'd be a little bit proud of me. He stared
straight ahead at the screen, stony-faced.

Then I started to improvise because I'd heard
that black lawyer bring up the Central Park jogger; I *had* to answer what he said, and that's when
it all fell apart. Even a day later, the way the
audience attacked me made me cringe. They
didn't want to listen to anything. Their minds
were already made up. Their chant of "A rape
is a rape!" sounded as though they were having
a good time; they were participating in a show,
and fact or fiction made no difference.

I listened to myself blubbering "you don't understand" over and over. I came across even worse than I'd thought. Mom and Dad watched with me to the end. It was painful.

Dad abruptly switched off the TV. "You shouldn't have been put through that." His jaw was clenched. "There was no reason for that." I could see that he was torn between anger at me and just plain hurt.

"I'm sorry," I whispered. I couldn't stand the look on his face. "I sounded like a fool."

"No you didn't," Mom said. "But the Delaneys had no business putting you up to it."

"It wasn't the Delaneys. *I* wanted to."

Mom shook her head, disgusted, but she didn't say anything. We were both worn out with arguments that didn't go anywhere.

It wasn't the Delaneys. Mr. Romano and the other lawyers were invited to be on the show to represent the boys' side and they all declined. "When you're preparing a case, there are too many things you can't say. I'd be muzzled," Mr. Romano explained. "It would be good if *someone* could do a little PR for the boys."

I volunteered. They didn't put me on the panel; they'd arranged to take my call. I was glad now that I hadn't been there with everyone looking at me. I'd wound up stunned and speechless as it was.

"I messed up," I said. "I should have faced them down."

"You spoke well," Dad said. "You wrote a good letter, too, I'll give you that. But I want you to stop with this now. Stop, do you hear me? Enough! Laura Jean, I want your promise."

I shook my head. "I won't make a promise like that."

Dad slammed his fist down on the couch and stalked out of the room. Mom looked at me, outraged. My throat started to hurt; I knew the next few days would be heavy silence.

This was the first time that I'd completely defied them, and there was nothing they could do. I kept going to Scott's no matter what Mom said. I was too old to be spanked and there was no way she could ground me; she had no control over me anymore.

"Do you have any idea of how upset your father is?" Mom said. "Do you even care?"

"I can't help it."

"We deserve better than this from you," Mom said. "We deserve better." She got up and left the room.

It was becoming yesterday's news; the reporters were no longer camped in front of the Delaneys'. I felt more comfortable there than in my own home.

"You were . . . *eloquent*," Mrs. Delaney said.

"I wish."

"You did fine." Mr. D put his arm around my shoulders. "There you were, a high school girl, speaking on national television as though you do it every single day. You were so natural and— Laura Jean, you came across natural and real."

"It had to help," Mrs. Delaney said. "It had to make people think."

Later, when Scott and I were alone in his room, he said, "My mother's in a dream world. Nothing's gonna help. What, you think a grand jury is gonna care that I go to church?"

He was right. That show was entertainment, that's all.

"It's Cara's word against ours. That's what it comes down to."

"Is that what Mr. Romano says?"

"Joe Lopez isn't that credible because he's on the team; everybody knows he's friends with us. Our best shot is the holes in Cara's story, like saying Charlie was there. And there wasn't a mark on her, no bruises, nothing. And there was an incident before, a couple of years back, when she was fooling around with some old man."

"She *was?* That's great, isn't it? That proves—"

"Romano says that's probably not admissible."

"But—"

"You know something? Romano charges two hundred twenty-five dollars an hour. He times every damn phone call. If this goes on and on, it could break my folks." He cleared his throat. "They're out to get us one way or the other. Romano says even if we didn't force her, they could still get us on rape if they decide she's not a consenting adult."

"That's not fair! She's eighteen! Isn't she?"

"They can say she's too retarded to know what she was doing. That's a load of bullshit! She might be dumb, but she sure as hell knew what she was doing! She loved it!"

"She's smart enough to take high school tests isn't she? I saw her there during finals."

Scott shrugged.

"When we started," I said, "I was only fifteer I wasn't a 'consenting adult' either."

"Hell, neither was I." Some of the old hum

came into his eyes. "You seduced me, L.J. Down-right corrupted me."

He hadn't made *love* to Cara; he hadn't been sweet-talking or kissing her. It was about as personal as Scott taking a leak, a physical blip. Mrs. Delaney was right; it was better not to think about it.

I reached for his hand. "The truth is on our side. It'll work out, you'll see."

"Do me a big favor, OK? No phony cheer. I'm getting all I can take from my mom."

I sat still next to him.

"The truth is, it looks bad," he said.

Endless silence, our eyes on each other. He could be railroaded right into jail. He knew it and I knew it. That would be the popular thing to do, I saw that on the Collins show. *My God, Scott didn't belong in jail! What would they do to him?*

My breath started coming in shallow pants and I couldn't stop. I was afraid I was going to hyperventilate. Pat had had an anxiety attack once; she'd almost blacked out from lack of oxygen. Think about something else. Air in. Air out.

I held tight to his hand. Find something, anything, to say. Breathe. OK. Slow and deep.

He raised my hand to his mouth. He nibbled

on my thumb. He sucked on the knuckle, and I watched his lips move and I thought, *Somehow, somewhere, I have to save him.*

No matter what, people continue with the motions of their normal lives. What else is there? Scott took his finals at home. Tommy spent a lot of time working on his trains in the basement. I don't know what the other guys were doing. I kept covering my Foodtown shifts.

It was the after-six rush. That's when a lot of customers stop in on their way home from work and the lines get almost as bad as on Saturdays. I was busy packing a big order. I always double-bag, I try to pack dairy items and frozen foods together, and I'm really careful about putting produce on top so it won't get squashed; a lot of the check-out girls don't bother. Some of the customers know that and deliberately go to my aisle. It makes me feel good; I like feeling competent, even if it's on a dumb job.

Anyway, I was bagging bottles of soda when I heard a brusque "You're Laura Jean Kettering, aren't you?" I looked up, surprised.

"Yes," I said. Two customers down—it took a second for the familiar face to click. Mrs. Snowden. Cara's mother.

She left her cart and pushed through toward me. "I read your letter. I read what you wrote."

I stood stock still, my hand still curled around a Pepsi.

"How could another girl—another *woman*—" Her voice was icy and tight. "What *are* you? Do you know what they did to my daughter?"

Everything around us stopped.

"How can you defend— Savages, all of you!" I'd never felt so much cold hatred directed at me. "Savages. You wrote—you wrote—not a shred of decency. She *admired* you. *You.* Laura Jean Kettering." She spit out my name like a curse.

Then Ted, the manager, was there. "What— *uh*—is there a problem here?"

"Oh no, there's no problem! No problem at all!" Strands of hair had worked loose from Mrs. Snowden's ponytail.

Everyone stared as she stalked out of the store.

"What was that about?" Ted said. "What happened?"

I shook my head.

The man I'd been packing for, a burly guy in a plaid shirt, shrugged. "She shoved right in front of the line."

"What— Shoot, she left a full cart!" Ted blew out a stream of air, exasperated.

The routine took over. Scanning, packing, Ted rolling the cart through the aisles and replacing groceries. I got a paper cut from a bag— occupational hazard—and my index finger smarted.

I was sorry for Mrs. Snowden, I really was. It had to be terrible to have the town slut for a daughter. But that was no excuse for making a public scene. For a moment there, I was afraid she'd physically attack me. She seemed deranged.

I dreaded going to bed that night. I couldn't sleep anymore, not all the way through.

When I was very young, maybe five or six, my parents took me to see a movie at the library one night. *Island of the Blue Dolphins.* Nice title, a children's movie from a children's book. Something about an Indian girl marooned on an island with wild dogs. The only part that I still remembered clearly was the wild dogs, snarling, growling, their teeth bared. After all those years, that was still vivid. I had nightmares about them for months afterward. Even awake, I imagined them in the dark, circling around the swing set under my window, creeping into my room. Daddy had to sit in my room every night until I finally fell asleep. Then I'd wake up with a start and find him gone, and he'd have to come and sit with me again. I remember Daddy, patient and bored, nodding off in the uncomfortable little chair at my desk. Maybe Mom sat with me, too; it's Daddy that I remember.

It passed and nothing like that ever happened again. Until now.

I needed to sleep. I fluffed the pillows and lay in bed, and tried to turn off my thoughts. I dozed off, exhausted. Then I was jolted awake, in a cold sweat. I sat upright in the dark, my heart pounding. I would have preferred slinking wild dogs to the blind terror that had become a nightly event.

I was Laura Jean Kettering, in my own room. The fluorescent glow was the clock on my desk. I made myself lie back. I smelled the scent of fabric softener on my pillowcase and I listened to the crickets outside, and my thoughts circled and circled.

Scott. Every trashy prison movie I'd ever seen unreeled before me. Perverts. The rape-in-the-shower scene. Sadistic guards.

Scott. Cara.

"She admired you," her mother had said. That was so odd. I didn't even know the girl existed until—

Cara had said, "Hi, Laura Jean," kind of hopefully, on the school stairs. Maybe—maybe if I acted friendly, she would talk to me. If I could get her to admit she was lying . . . But how would I prove . . . *Tape!* Get her talking and tape it! It was a long shot, but maybe there was a chance . . .

JOE LOPEZ

I was helping Coach Barrett close up the equipment room for the summer.

"Are we supposed to bring the blocking dummies in?" I asked.

"No, no, they can stay out." Coach seemed distracted and quiet, with none of the usual stories or kidding around.

We had put in a good morning's work. There was a lot of jumbled stuff to sort out. Coach made a list of what needed to be replaced for next year.

"No one respects property anymore," he said. "These things could last another couple of seasons if someone took the least bit of care. Lucky we get a good budget."

After a game, we'd just throw things in, too psyched up to think about the equipment. We came off the field like warriors from battle, bruised and triumphant. Best high in the world.

We worked alongside each other, quiet.

The Shorehaven Kings. We'd been *something!* I'd miss it.

We were oiling the last of the baseball gloves when Coach said, "What happened, Joe? What happened to my boys?"

I didn't know how to answer him.

"Sure, I wanted my team to win, but— I know how some of the other coaches— But I thought I was building character. Molding boys into men."

I concentrated on the dry cracks in the mitt in my hand.

"I tried," he said.

"You did, Coach. You made us into a team, all for one and one for all, remember? Like, maybe Clay and I didn't get along so great, but I always trusted him to come through for me in a game. Like, we had loyalty; we stood up for each other if anybody tried to mess with us. We hung out together. We prayed together before the games, remember?"

He slowly shook his head. "I left out compassion."

"Football did a lot for me," I said.

"Mrs. Barrett and I had a couple in for dinner the other night. The wife was French. She couldn't understand our system, all that emphasis on sports in the schools, athletic scholarships. Confused values, she said. A couple of months ago, I could have given her a good argument . . ."

"Sports is the only thing that keeps a lot of guys in school," I said.

"I had them for four years." He was rubbing the oiled rag on the leather, over and over, in the same spot. "I thought I knew them."

"Kids are more careful around teachers and parents. Even around you, Coach."

"Why were you the one that walked away from it, Joe? Why you and not the others?"

I wanted to give him an honest answer. There was that moment when we were all breathing together like one thing. And then I peeled off.

"I'm not sure. I guess I'm more like a loner," I said. "The things they did after I left, though. The mop. I never would've gone along with that. I know that much about myself."

"Talk to me, Joe. I need to know."

"I thought Cara Snowden was a pig. But I wouldn't do that to anybody. I just wouldn't."

"Go on."

His erect posture was gone. He looked like an old man. I didn't like seeing that.

"Dan Gregory's the one you ought to be talking to." He was a better man than me. That was the truth. "Me?" I shrugged. "I love being with a woman, that's my scene, Coach. But what they did had nothing to do with wanting a woman, not as far as I can see."

He took the last of the gloves and placed them neatly on the shelf.

"I guess we're finished here," he said. "Thanks."

"You had no control off the field. Their families are supposed to be the ones teaching them right from wrong."

He shook his head. "Dietrich. Bob Dietrich." He switched off the light. "Delaney . . ."

I opened the door. I held it and waited for him.

"That's OK. You go on, Joe. I'll stay here a while."

The last I saw him, he was sitting on the bench, alone, his arms hanging loosely at his sides.

LAURA JEAN

THE MECHANICS OF IT WERE SIMPLE. MY TAPE recorder fit easily into my tan slouch bag. All I'd have to do was slip my hand under the leather flap and feel for the "on" button. I experimented, recording from four feet away. "Testing, one, two, three, testing." With the top of the bag open and the recorder tilted up, it was OK. Not the greatest sound quality in the world, but clear enough.

The tough part would be finding Cara; I couldn't exactly call her at home. Classes were over now, with graduation and the damn Fling set for next Saturday. Anyway, I'd heard she'd been pulled out of Shorehaven, except for her finals.

The first place I looked was the high school track. Cara was a runner, and runners run, I thought, whether the season is over or not, just like the basketball players walk through town dribbling a ball, just like Scott keeps taking slap shots against the garage door with a rubber puck.

As I walked to the track that afternoon, I felt strong and charged with energy. Even the leaves on the trees seemed a brighter green. It felt good to be *doing* something.

There were a few lone runners trotting around the circle. No blonds. Anne Pierce and Valerie-something were stretching at the entrance. They were sophomores, but I knew Anne from Ski Club last winter.

"Hi, what's up?" I said.

"Hi."

"What are you guys doing? Track team still practicing?"

"*Uh-uh*, the last meet was a week ago Tuesday."

"Cara Snowden was on the team, right?"

"She used to be."

"Has she been coming out to the track?"

"No, she's not *allowed*." Valerie laughed. "That's what she said."

"Oh."

"Are you looking for her, Laura Jean?" Both girls stared at me curiously. Of course. They knew I was Scott's girlfriend.

So I couldn't pull off *subtle*; what difference

did it make? "Yes," I said. "Where would I find her?"

"I don't know." Anne shrugged. "We don't hang out with her or anything."

"What're you going to do to her?" Valerie said, round-eyed with excitement.

"Nothing. I want to talk to her, that's all."

"I saw her this morning," Valerie said. "You know that dirt road past Henderson? Just before you get to the beach? I guess she runs there because"—Valerie snorted a laugh—"because her mommy won't *allow* her on the track."

It took two false-start mornings of waiting around the mouth of that back road, checking and rechecking the tape recorder, frustrated and waiting. On the third morning, there she was, coming around the bend.

She was alone, running toward me. I placed myself in her path.

"Hi, Cara!" I can't imagine what my smile looked like; I'm not that great an actress.

She stopped, one foot poised to take off.

"Cara?" I came closer and she flinched. People must have been giving her a hard time.

"I was going to run, too," I said, "but it's so hot. You want to take a break for a while and hang out?"

"Hang out?" She looked at me uncertainly.

My mind was racing. "Come on, Cara. Let's go to McCall's and have some shakes. My treat." McCall's was empty in the daytime, cool and quiet. I could place the bag between us in a booth—but why would she go anywhere with me? I must have been dreaming.

"I'm not allowed. I'm supposed to go straight home."

"Do you do everything your mom says?"

"I don't have to," she mumbled, eyes on the ground.

"I thought we'd hang out and talk, you know—" I sounded like an idiot. I'd never even spoken to the girl before; I didn't know anything about her. Except that I hated her.

She was scraping lines in the ground with her sneaker, head down, shoulders curved forward. At least she wasn't leaving.

Nobody from school wanted anything to do with her; she had to be lonesome. "I thought— *uh*—I thought you might want some company."

"You're not mad at me?" she asked.

I shook my head. "No, of course not."

"We're friends, right?" she asked hesitantly.

"Sure."

She looked so happy.

CARA

I'm walking to McCall's with Laura Jean
Kettering. Laura Jean Kettering said, "Let's go
to McCall's." It's like we always go places and
hang out and stuff. Like we're best friends.

"I like your hair," I say. "The way it waves
on the side."

"Thanks."

"How do you get it to go like that? I like the
color, too."

I pull my ponytail out of the ribbon. I fluff
out my hair.

"I only tie it back when I run," I tell her, "so
it doesn't get in my eyes. I like mine loose,
too."

I think she'll say it's pretty, but she doesn't.

"I always have my ribbons match my shorts.
I just got new shorts. They're Calvins. My mom
got them on sale and it was so lucky. There was
just one pair left and they were my size!"

"That was pretty lucky," Laura Jean says.

"They're yellow and they have two pockets in the back. Mommy bought them right away. At Macy's at Roosevelt Field. I didn't go with her. I don't know why, because I like Roosevelt Field. You know the store that has those giant cookies? The soft ones? Across from where the bookstore is? Anyway, she took a chance, because you can't return on sale. And they fit me perfect! I wear size eight. It was pretty lucky. What's your favorite color?"

"*Uh*—green."

"Pink is my favorite, but green is my second favorite." I'll tell Mommy to buy me something green. "Anyway, they're not bright yellow. They're like faded yellow. Calvins are so cool. They're cool, right?"

Laura Jean nods and smiles when I tell her things. She's my friend. When I used to walk home from track with Anne, she said, "Stop talking so much." Anyway, that was before.

The air-conditioning is on at McCall's. It's dark at first when you come in from outside. I'm sweaty from running and now my arms feel cold.

Next time *I'll* say, "Let's go to McCall's. My treat." Maybe tomorrow. Maybe sometime we'll go to Dominic's and have pizza. Me and Laura Jean Kettering.

"Let's take a booth," Laura Jean says. I go in first and she slides in next to me.

"I love shakes," I say. "What's your favorite flavor?"

"Oh. I guess, chocolate," she says.

"Me, too. Chocolate's my favorite, too!"

The waiter comes and Laura Jean orders two chocolate shakes for us.

"In ice cream, I like Rocky Road best, but once I bit down and chipped my front tooth, I had to go to the dentist to get it fixed, see, right here."

Laura Jean looks at my tooth. "Oh. That's too bad."

"That was at my daddy's, in New Jersey. I have a baby brother, he's so cute, you know what he did? He was playing he was a fish in the bathtub and he splashed the water everyplace. It was all over the floor."

I like talking to somebody. A teenager like me. It's not fun with Mommy. A lot of kids are mean to me. Kids I don't even know. When they pass me on the street, they yell things. About the mop and bottle. I don't listen. I don't mind that much. I don't listen.

Laura Jean laughs. "He sounds cute, Cara."

Laura Jean Kettering is popular and she likes me.

The shakes come and we sip them through the straws.

"My little brother, his name is Joey. He's so funny when I play with him. He likes when I tickle." I haven't been to Daddy's for a long time. I miss Daddy and Joey. "I like babies and little things, like baby bunnies and . . . I hope my mom will let me get a kitten. She might. I'll be so gentle. I like kittens a whole lot."

"I have a cat named Muffin," Laura Jean says.

"That's such a cute name! I like cats."

Laura Jean says, "You like boys, too, don't you, Cara?"

"*Uh-huh.*" I look away and twist my straw. I hope she doesn't want to make fun of me. About what happened with the boys.

"Me, too." Laura Jean leans over and giggles. "Let's talk about boys. Who do you like?"

She just wants to talk about boys the way girls do. Because we're friends.

"Who do you like, Cara?"

I twist and twist the straw. "I don't know," I say.

"I bet you like *somebody*," she says. "Come

on, no secrets. Tell me the truth now, who do you like?"

I wish I had somebody to like and talk about. "You're so lucky you're Scott's girlfriend." I stir my shake with the straw because it's thicker on the bottom. "I wish I was you."

LAURA JEAN

I'D PLACED MY BAG ON THE SEAT BETWEEN US.
The shadow of the table partly covered it. The
lighting in McCall's was dim.

She'd been going on and on, as if a dam had
burst. Her face was animated. There was something terribly off-kilter. Disconnected. About
shorts and her brother and kittens . . . All I
wanted was to get done with it.

I strained to be casual; I found myself picking
up her tone, talking kindergarten conversation.
I wasn't prepared for anything like this.

And then, "You're so lucky you're Scott's girlfriend," she said.

She brought up his name by herself! An
opening!

"I wish I was you," she said.

"What? Me?"

"They're not nice to me anymore."

My hand snaked into my bag. OK, *here we
go*, I thought.

"Just between us—Scott is really handsome, isn't he?" I said.

"He's the second most handsome after Bob. Oh—do you mind my saying he's second?" She looked worried, eager to please. She wasn't what I had expected at all. I had imagined someone wild and tougher.

I pushed the "on" button.

"You like Scott," I said. "That's OK, I don't blame you." I was too nervous. This could be my only shot. "I would have picked him, too. When they said, 'Who do you want,' did you point at him? Come on, I'm your friend, you can tell me. Did you pick Scott?" I held my breath. I was pushing too hard.

"*Uh-huh.* You're not mad, right?"

"No. Tell me about it, Cara."

"About what?" She was looking all around McCall's, in every direction.

"Cara. About that afternoon. You and the boys and—and Scott."

She shook her head.

"Oh, come on. I thought we were friends. I just want to know the way it happened. Just between us."

She wouldn't look at me. She was moving restlessly in the booth. I was losing her.

I took another sip of my shake. The tape was running, running. Recording silence.

"I love parties," I said, "don't you?"

She turned toward me. *"Uh-huh."*

"I love dancing. You were dancing that afternoon, weren't you? It sounds like so much fun. You took your clothes off and danced and stuff? I'm your friend, you can tell me. You know, just girl to girl."

Her face opened up. "It was so much fun! They were clapping and everything. Scott said, 'Do a strip, Cara. We're all friends here.' Before, he was telling me things to say with the F-word and we laughed so hard. It was so funny."

Scott!

"We were kidding around and everything. Me and the guys."

I forced a giggle. "I wish I'd been there. It sounds like fun."

"That part. At the beginning."

"How about later?"

She didn't answer.

"Did you say 'no' later?" I realized my nails were digging into my palm. "When they—when they screwed you, did you say 'no' to anybody?"

"I was nice to them so they'd like me. It was nice the time with Bob, the time in the woods."

I had her!

"You did it in the woods with Bob?"

"Bob Dietrich. He was going to be my boy-friend."

"He was?" A cold shiver was creeping up my back.

"We'd have hung out with you and Scott, right? It would have been nice, right?"

I closed my eyes. I didn't know; she was like a five-year-old. I didn't know.

"It would have been nice," I answered.

She sighed. "I wish like anything it had been like that."

The tape was running. I had programmed myself to do this; I went on with it. Closing in for the kill. "Cara, that afternoon—the mop handle. Did you like that?"

"No." She turned away.

"Cara, did you say 'no' about the mop—"

"Scott said it would be exciting, they said I'd like it, but it hurt. They said try it, you'll like it. They were my friends and they wanted me to."

My stomach turned over and the tape was running and I was stuck on automatic. "Did you ever say 'no' that afternoon? Cara, did anyone ever keep you from leaving?"

"No."

I wanted to shake her. "Didn't you do anything to stop them? Why didn't you try to get away?"

"No. I don't know. I didn't know what I was supposed to do."

"So you just went along with it? Oh, God!"

"I guess . . ."

"Oh, Cara! Why didn't you—"

"Laura Jean? Does Scott hurt you when he—you know?"

I pushed the "off" button. I felt sick. "I have to go." I grabbed my bag and dropped some bills on the table. "Sorry. I have to go. I'm sorry."

Her voice trailed after me. "Are you mad, Laura Jean? I didn't mean to tell on him."

I managed to make it home before I started throwing up.

I was glad no one was home to hear. I couldn't stop retching. I leaned on the sink; it was cold against my arm. My stomach kept heaving long after there was nothing left.

I rinsed my mouth with Lavoris and I washed my face. Afterwards, I rested on my bed. Maybe there was nothing at all on the tape. Maybe it had jammed. I pulled the recorder out of my bag.

Cara's breathy little-girl words were distinct. My voice, warm and clear, kept repeating, "I'm your friend; you can tell me."

She had no defenses at all. I could have manipulated her into anything.

I didn't know. I didn't know!

Cara was in Tommy's class in second grade. Scott must have been on the same school bus for all those elementary school years. Dietrich, too, in the same neighborhood school. And Dan Gregory.

I tasted vomit in my mouth.

I couldn't block it out anymore. They had been like cats toying with a mouse, playing with her, using their power over her for laughs on a slow afternoon. Scott would have been one of the leaders, I was certain of that; I couldn't fool myself into believing it was uncharacteristic. Some of the boys might have been passive onlookers. Joe Lopez walked away from it. Dan Gregory stuck his neck way out to put a stop to it. And Scott was a leader.

That's who Scott Delaney was. It was in the same stew with all the qualities that I loved. But this was a chunk that would stick in my throat and choke me.

I'd raped Cara Snowden a second time, and

now I had my precious tape. *I could erase it,* I thought. No one would ever know. Except me.

I called on the saints of my childhood. I wished I was a little girl again, with nothing more pressing than giving up Hershey Bars for Lent. I was Joan of Arc without any voices and in possession of a hot tape.

It was true, there had been no physical violence. I couldn't let Scott go down for something he *didn't* do. I owed him that much. Let the grand jury deal with what he *did* do that afternoon.

I called Mr. Romano.

"He's in a meeting right now," his secretary said. "May I take a message?"

"This is Laura Jean Kettering, Scott Delaney's friend. It's important. Please, tell him it's urgent."

I paced. Finally, he called back. I told him, a garble of words spilling out.

"Wait, let me understand this," he said. "The Snowden girl did not know she was being recorded?"

"Yes. I mean, she didn't know."

"If it's her voice alone, that's not admissible. It could be admissible if it's part of a conversation with someone else, someone who was aware of it and acquiescent. Now, tell me. Was there such a conversation?"

"Well, yes. I was talking to her."

"Your voice is on the tape?"

"Yes."

"OK."

"It was just me—does that make it OK?"

"You recorded your own conversation; you were a willing participant."

"Oh."

"You should know you were interfering with a witness; that's obstruction of justice. Now, I haven't seen the tape, I haven't heard it, I don't know if there's anything of value on it. At this moment, I have no proof that it actually exists. Once you hand over this alleged tape to me, I'm free to make it public."

"Does that mean I'll be in trouble?"

"I doubt it would amount to more than a slap on the wrist. I certainly didn't put you up to it; I assume no one else did."

"No."

"You're absolutely sure Scott didn't plan this?"

"He didn't know anything about it. I didn't want to get his hopes up . . ."

"All right, good."

I hesitated for just a moment. "I'll get it to you, Mr. Romano."

LAURA JEAN

I SENT THE PACKAGE TO MR. ROMANO. Registered mail, return receipt requested. I had intended to stop at the Delaneys on the way back from the post office, but I couldn't make myself do it.

I waited a day.

Finally I forced my feet up the front path, past the lamppost with THE DELANEYS in wrought-iron script. A branch of the hydrangea brushed my shoulder. It needed to be trimmed. By August, it would be covered with bright blue blooms. I remembered when the worn-away plastic daisies on the doormat had been new.

Scott bear hugged me when I came in. "Hey, babe, where've you been?"

It would have felt natural to let myself fall into his arms. Instead, I told him about the tape.

Scott was elated. "She admitted she was lying! That's great! That's great!"

"Not in those words. She said she'd never tried to get away. She'd never said 'no.' "

"Same thing. That's the best"—he grabbed for me—"L.J., you're the best!"

"The best at what?"

He picked up on the edge in my tone. The big smile faded. "What do you mean? What's the matter?"

I didn't know how to start. It was so hard.

"You look like hell. What— Is something wrong?"

We were standing in his front hall. The console with the painting of oranges over it, the orange plaid runner, the basket where they kept their mail, the full-length mirror, the smell of Windex. I memorized everything.

"L.J., what happened? Did someone say something to you?" He put his arm around my shoulders protectively. He was like that; he'd go after anyone who'd insulted me.

"L.J.?"

This was Scott. The stray strands of thick hair over his forehead. No matter how much he brushed them back, they would never stay.

He watched me and waited.

I didn't know how to say it but to say it. "I did this last thing for you. And that's all. I'm through."

His arm dropped from my shoulders. "What do you mean, through?"

I looked away. I felt awkward, unaccountably embarrassed. "We're finished. We're over." My voice floated in the air, in words that I wouldn't take back.

"OK, OK, what are you mad about?"

"I'm not," I said. "But I know how it was with Cara now."

"I don't get it. Hey, you just got proof I was telling the truth. No one forced her."

"I know, you didn't have to. God, all I needed to say to her was 'I'm your friend.' " I tried to keep my voice steady. "It had to be so easy. I can't wipe that out. Scott, I really can't. Even if I tried—I can't. I can't do it."

"What did she say to you? She's been telling you lies, that's all. What did she say?"

"The way she looked at me . . . She'd trust anybody who said something nice to her. She doesn't know, she can't tell the difference between . . . It was too easy. She's defenseless. And you went ahead and . . . I can't be with you anymore. I can't."

"You can't be with me?" he said incredulously.

I nodded. His face swam before my eyes.

"On account of Cara? That's crazy. Cara's *nothing!*"

"No. No, she's a person."

"Oh, come on, you know what I mean."

"She was a thing for you to play with. You had fun. You and the boys."

"I thought we had that all settled," he said. "I told you; I didn't make *love* to her, L.J."

"It's not because you had sex," I said. "That's not what I'm talking about."

"So what's the problem?"

"You knew she was retarded. You and Tommy. And Bob. You all went to the same elementary school. You must have seen her on the school bus all those years. You knew all about her."

"So?"

"So maybe rape isn't the name for it. Maybe it's called child abuse."

"Wait a minute. OK, talking to her got you shook up. I can understand that but, hey, you're going way overboard with this. Come on, forget about her. Don't think about it."

"I don't want to forget about her. I don't want to think it's all right. That's not who I want to be. I'm through, Scott. I really am."

"I don't believe this," he said. "You're not doing this. Not because of her."

"It matters."

"I love you, L.J. What do you want me to say? What do you want me to do?"

I shook my head. The orange plaid of the rug blurred in front of me.

"I treated you like a queen," he said. "I always treated you right, didn't I?"

He had made me happy. A little while ago, I would have done just about anything to keep him. Not all that different from Cara. The difference of some IQ points.

"She's 'the other,' isn't she?" I said.

"What's that supposed to mean?"

"Would you be cruel to a retarded *boy*, too? Or was it because she's a *woman* and retarded? You used to say that thing about women being goddesses or doormats. Oh wow, I was so glad you put me in the right category! Well, people aren't goddesses. And they're not doormats, either."

"I don't get what you're talking about."

"I know you don't."

"Were you asking me would I screw a boy? Hell, no! What kind of question is that?"

We stared at each other. His eyes, his mouth, his nose—I saw disconnected features and couldn't manage to join them together.

"I've still got some of my stuff here," I finally

said. "My black heels, and I left my dress in Ginny's closet." I had changed after the Sports Awards Dinner. I was happy that night. "I'll have someone come by to pick it up later."

This felt like an amputation. Without anesthesia.

"You don't end it like that—*snap!* That's crazy," he said.

"I know how I feel. I know what I think. There's nothing left to talk about." I wasn't good at this. I was hurting myself, but I plunged on. "We're over."

We stood there, not saying anything, for the longest time. I couldn't look directly into his eyes. Minutes, years, ticked by. Over. The end.

"Shit," he said. He looked boyish and defeated.

I had done it. I opened the door and, like a sleepwalker, went through.

He caught me on the front path and whirled me around. "OK, what's the real reason? Did your folks finally get to you? Is that it?"

"No! I just about gave them up for you! Didn't you hear anything I said?"

His mouth twisted. "A rat deserting a sinking ship."

"Don't, Scott. Don't trash everything." My voice broke. "I stood by you."

"Yeah, sure."

"You know I did! I shafted Cara for you. I delivered that stinking tape, didn't I? I loved you. I *loved* you! I tried every which way not to see—"

He reached for me. I stepped back before he could touch me.

"I need you, Elly. I'm not off the hook yet and— You've picked one hell of a time, just when I—"

"No," I said. "It won't work."

We were standing apart, facing each other. I felt disembodied, unreal. I didn't belong to anyone anymore.

"I hope it turns out all right for you," I said thickly. "And—well, I guess—that's all."

He stared at me blankly.

Then, bitter and mocking, "Did you find yourself a date for the Fling? Are you gonna get to wear your *pretty dress?*"

A lawn mower across the street sputtered and started up again.

"Good-bye, Scott," I said.

LAURA JEAN

IT HAD BEEN UNSEASONABLY WARM ALL SPRING. Graduation morning was hot and humid. We clustered in the gym to get our black gowns and caps. The gowns covered shorts and T-shirts, and suddenly everyone looked different, a sea of black. I felt leaden in the midst of the buzz of excitement.

There was an occasional glimpse of bare leg as the folds whirled. It wasn't necessary to be dressed up underneath; almost everyone would go straight home from graduation to get ready for the Fling that night.

Pat, next to me, was bubbling. "I'm getting a facial and my nails wrapped, the only appointment I could get is for three, so I'll have to rush like crazy to make it for cocktails at—" She suddenly stopped herself. "Oh. I'm sorry, L.J."

"It's OK. It doesn't matter," I said. I had a vision of emerald green silk whirling around my legs, my face radiant and somehow regal with

my hair in a French knot, and Scott, sophisti-
cated in a dinner jacket, holding my arm. It was
so real I could have touched it.

"It doesn't matter," I repeated. It seemed in-
credible that I had wanted to manipulate Dad
out of money he couldn't afford for one stupid
dress.

"Everybody, line up! Come on, it's time!"

The band had started and we came out onto
the field. Step-stop, step-stop. I saw my parents
and Anne and Teresa in the stands. My other
sister Mary lives in Seattle. Mom waved and I
smiled back. Mom and Dad were pleased with
me again. For their sake, I hoped I wouldn't be
hauled into a courtroom. But I'd do whatever I
had to do. I wasn't theirs anymore, not in the
same way.

We filed into the mass of chairs on the field.
"Pomp and Circumstance" ended and the last
few scrambled into their seats.

The invocation and then the speakers. ". . . As
you go out into the world . . ." It was hot under
the cap. I knew my face was getting shiny.
". . . Your formative years at Shorehaven High
School . . ."

I felt light, unanchored. Without Scott. What
had my "formative years" been all about?

The gown was itchy against my bare arms.

I listened to bits and pieces of the speeches. ". . . fulfilling the promise of . . . It is up to you, as you take your places . . . You are our bright hopes for tomorrow . . ."

The kids around me were squirming restlessly in their seats, signaling to their friends. They were too hyped up to be patient through the endless words. I was out of sync. Unattached and detached. Bare-wristed. I had forgotten to return the bracelet. It was no good to him. My name was on it; he couldn't give it to another girl. Well, I'd send it to him, anyway.

The valedictorian spoke. ". . . all that our parents and our teachers have instilled . . . with honor and faith in . . . and four years of friendships that we will always remember."

I didn't know the valedictorian from Adam; *smart* didn't cut it here. If brains had been the way to be popular, we'd all have been jockeying to be nuclear physicists. I had majored in Pretty.

Finally, Mr. Gilmartin. "It is with great pride that I . . ." We were called individually for the diplomas. The line snaked toward the podium. The missing names echoed in my head: Scott Delaney. Bob Dietrich. John Masci. Mike Clay. Tim Hughes. There were raucous cheers when Charlie Goren was called. A good round of applause for Joe Lopez. My turn came; Mr. Gilmartin handed the diploma to me and shook my hand. "Laura Jean!" "Yeah, L.J.!" I was one of the popular ones. Another missing name: Dan Gregory. He'd have his diploma mailed to him, I thought, and get out of Shorehaven and never come back. I was sorry I never got to know him better.

I couldn't help getting caught up in the exhilaration of throwing our caps in the air. Friends and family streamed onto the field. Through the confusion, I saw Joe Lopez surrounded by his family, three girls and a glowing mother. The littlest sister was hanging on his arm, all over him, and he swung her around, laughing.

Then Teresa and Anne worked their way toward me, Dad hugged me, Mom beamed. I smiled brightly until it almost felt real, and high school was over.